Introduction

'Is that a gun in your pocket, or are you just pleased to see me?'

'A hard man is good to find.'

'Goodness, what beautiful diamonds.' . . . 'Goodness had nothing to do with it, dearie.'

'Climbing the career ladder, wrong by wrong.'

'It's better to be looked over than overlooked.'

'Between two evils, I always pick the one I never tried before.'

'When I'm good, I'm very, very good, but when I'm bad I'm better.'

Lines like this have had audiences reeling from quip-lash for much of the twentieth century. Mae West had a black belt in the art of tongue-fu.

And then there's the body. Famous for breasts which arrived five minutes before *she* did, the Battle of Britain pilots named their inflatable chest life preservers 'Mae Wests'. From the makeshift airstrips in Egyptian deserts and Pacific islands, airmen flew into battle with her legs splay-painted on their fuselages, whilst beneath the waves those same legs trembled on the tattooed musculature of sailors manning allied submarines. And her lips – Salvador Dali designed a sofa of red silk made from enlarged photographs of Mae's mouth.

But apart from The Body, which makes every other female feel like a bag full of cold porridge, and The Wit, which should have been registered at Police Head-quarters as a lethal weapon, what do we *really* know about her?

Mae West was born in 1893, the progeny of an unlikely coupling of a society beauty and a streetfighter nicknamed Battlin' Jack. By the time she died in 1980, her minestrone mix of talent had made her a successful comedienne, singer, dancer, playwright, director, actress, scriptwriter, producer, Sex Goddess and novelist. If this isn't enough to make any writer impale herself on her pen, Mae was also a feminist who makes Madonna look like Julie Andrews, an intellectual who rubbed shoulder pads with the Roosevelts (this woman plucked her highbrows) and a civil libertarian who went to jail in defence of freedom of expression.

To cap it all, she was a brilliant business woman, who insisted on creative control: she refused to sign any Hollywood contract unless it contained a clause that the completed film must in every way be 'to her satisfaction'. Today, when the only creative muscle exercised by cinema stars is in their control-top panty-hose and screen-writers are the most put-upon of literary prostitutes, we can only marvel at a woman who invented the 'droit morale' in her contracts with Paramount for the films she wrote (including *Night After Night, I'm No Angel, Belle of the Nineties* and *Goin' to Town*).

To me, what makes Mae West so fas-cin-at-in', apart from the fact that she left school at twelve (having left school myself at fifteen – the only examination I've ever passed is my pap test – I like nothing more than discovering autodidacts) is that she accomplished all this in an era when women were meant to be no more than decorative and domestic. West may have been decorative but her domesticity was limited to the sewing of wild oats and barbecuing of sacred cows – entire *herds*. All this makes Mae West worthy of re-discovery. Suddenly, her feminism seems no longer precocious, but a precursor of how it should be, in an age where women demand to be treated as equals instead of sequels.

Mae made her stage debut at five, eluding the watchdogs of the Gerry Society, a child protection agency whose unexpected theatre visits would send little Buster Keaton scuttling into the nearest trunk. It was the time of 'Mr Bojangles', when a pre-tramp Charlie Chaplin was playing society drunks in imported London music hall acts, Groucho Marx was so young he was painting on his moustache and W.C. Fields (later her co-star in *My Little Chickadee*) had not yet contracted bottle-fatigue. These were her competitors, as she battled to keep out of the chorus and to rise to the top of the vaudeville bill.

It was also a time when women did not have the vote and mathematics was the main method of birth control. (Females who miscalculated in this ovarian roulette were called 'Mum'.) Margaret Sanger, an American midwife forbidden from studying to become a doctor, had to go to Holland to gather contraceptive information which she then published in pamphlet form in 1912. They were banned under Post Office legislation designed to prevent obscene material being sent through the post. In most American states, women were not allowed to testify in court, hold title to property, establish businesses, take out bank loans or sign papers as witnesses. Wedlock was little more than a padlock, with wives compelled to pledge obedience. 'Insanity' and 'moral unfitness' were grounds for men to divorce their wives, depriving them of their children and casting them forth from marriage bed to Bedlam. Most females faced an anorexic range of occupations: badly paid domestic or factory work for the poor and badly paid teaching or nursing for the better educated. Denied equal pay or equal access to education and the professions (Harvard Law School only admitted women in the 1950s) a woman's economic dependence on her man in the early twentieth century kept her tethered to the tea towel.

When it came to morality, the majority of men were Olympic Gold Medal Champions in Double Standards. Hypocrisy in sexual relations was endemic, in literature as much as in life. Pre-marital sex labelled a man as a 'man' . . . and a female as a 'fallen woman', (in most cases, of course, she didn't fall, but was pushed). In books, sex was done in brackets. Foreplay, which consisted of lighting someone else's cigarette, was followed by an interval of asterisks. Women didn't have orgasms, they had a row of dots . . .

Mae West fought the hypocrisy of the times with the only weapon available to her: shooting from the lip. She maintains that she became a writer by the accident of 'needing material and having no place to get it'. When producers found this material too controversial, she produced the plays herself. Her first play, which she wrote, directed and starred in, was coolly and simply called *Sex*. It was a smash hit on Broadway in 1926, even though New York newspapers were too prudish to accept advertisements for it. In it's forty-first sell-out week at Daly's theatre, it was raided by police, who sympathetically offered not to prosecute if she closed the play down. Mae chose to stand trial, courageously, as no court in the America of this prohibition era could be seen to tolerate immorality. The District Attorney had to concede that there was nothing lewd or lascivious in her script and that it was 'Miss West's personality, looks, walk, mannerisms and gestures which make the lines and situations suggestive' – especially her famous dance, the 'shimmy'. Just as Lenny Bruce, forty years later, was to claim that the obscenity was not in his act, but in the act of police officers who performed it in the witness box, so Mae West objected to being tried by hearsay.

She insisted on performing her 'shimmy' in the well of the court.

But obscenity is in the groin of the beholder. Mae's judge convicted her for 'corrupting the morals of youth', fined her $500 and sentenced her to a short spell on Devil's Island. She complained about her rough prison underwear and saw enough of homosexuality to write her next play about it, *The Drag*. The theatre management became nervous and asked for re-writes. Rather than dip her pen in disinfectant, West withdrew the play. But she was enough of a drawcard for the Biltmore Theatre to stage her next play, *The Pleasure Man* in 1928. Opening night saw an unscheduled third act: a team of New York's finest, brandishing their nightsticks, rushed on stage and arrested the entire cast. 'Mae West in Paddy wagon again' blared the headlines at the time, 'Bad Girl of Broadway in Trouble Once More'.

The instigator of this trouble was a fun-loving body called 'The Society for the Suppression of Vice', part of the 'moral purity' movement which was enormously powerful in America in the 20s. When it came to moral victories, these people were warmongers. The champagne-saturated, charlstoning image of America just before the Great Depression is historically false: the times were pious beyond belief. Mainstream America belonged to the bible-basher, campaigning against whisky and prostitution and demanding a rigid code of sexual behaviour from men and women alike. Many of these thin-lipped sexual McCarthyites were women who actually thought of themselves as 'feminists'. Ostensibly, the object of their concern was the young single woman who was now able to find work as a secretary or typist in cities on the East coast. A wholesome caricature of the new independent woman soon appeared: The Gibson Girl. She was dressed in a mannish blouse with a little tie at the high neck, a long dark skirt, glasses and 'follow me home and play scrabble' shoes. Always depicted as intensely serious, this woman couldn't crack a smile at a joke festival.

Mae West was her antithesis, and ultimately her antidote.

Through the seismic days of the Wall Street Crash, the gruelling Great Depression and the struggling New Deal, Mae West first mounted and stayed on her unique pedestal: an icon who raised eyebrows for a living. The box office declared her 'not guilty' on the grounds that the US Supreme Court was later to recognise as a defence to obscenity – she had a 'redeeming social purpose'. She combined sexuality with satire, at a time when America desperately needed a cure for it's irony-deficiency.

'I could say almost anything, do almost anything on a stage,' West reveals in her autobiography, 'if I smiled and was properly ironic in delivering my dialogue.'

It was this irresistible mix of sexuality and self-mockery which allowed Mae West to indulge her amorous philanthropy – 'Men are my kind of people, a favourite hobby' – and yet escape the social stigma of having what would be called these days 'margarine legs' – easily spread. Her dialogue was, moreover, a breath of fresh, one-liner-ed air beside the formalised heroines of the silent screen and the romantic tosh that crackled from sound tracks when they started to talk: a kind of verbal musak. As F. Scott Fitzgerald put it, 'In a world of Garbos, Barrymores, Harlowes, Valentinos and Clara Bows, Mae West is the only type with an ironic edge, a comic spark, that takes on a more cosmopolitan case of life's enjoyments.'

Reading between the lines of her autobiography, Mae's idea of fidelity was to only have one man in bed at a time. 'Getting down to your last man must be as bad as getting down to your last dollar.' Her obsession seemed to border on sexual kleptomania. 'Sometimes it seems to me I've known so many men that the FBI ought to come to me first to compare fingerprints.'

Perhaps she was just living down to her reputation. But in a letter to Dr Kinsey, of Kinsey Report fame, she struck an authentic note, 'Because I portray sex with humour and good nature instead of something shameful, I think my portrayals are accepted in the spirit in which I play them. I have excited and stimulated, but I have never demoralised.'

What a world away from the pornobabes of today, who wink and blush and masturbate into the vaselined lenses of 'glamour' photographers, or who bake their airbrushed brains on the beaches of 'Baywatch'. During the Gulf War, the US Air Force showed hard-core movies to stoke its A-10 pilots up before they took off to blast the Iraqis (and occasionally their allies). I prefer to think of the men in their Spitfires and Kittyhawks and Hurricanes, Mae Wests around their shoulders, her skirt blown up behind their propellers. Mae West not only rescued sex from the prudery of the Gibson Girls, she positively gave it a good name.

When it came to work, West contracted a healthy dose of *sceptic*-aemia where Hollywood was concerned, 'I always held it at arm's length like a would-be-lover one didn't fully trust.' About her plays she said that they were 'soon finished, remembered only by photographs and yellowing reviews.' Whereas 'a book lasts as long as someone keeps it on a shelf.' What makes Mae West a good novelist, besides the verbal callisthenics and triple entendres, is the rhythm of her prose, her vivid characterisation and sharp ear for dialogue. As she said of herself, 'I ain't 'fraid of pushin' grammar around so long as it sounds good.'

Babe Gordon, the female protagonist of 'The Constant Sinner', is, as critics at the time stated, 'The kind of woman every man wants to meet – at least once'. Mae West wrote the novel in 1937, adapting it to the screen and playing the role of Babe Gordon. Half a century later, Babe has not yet passed her amuse-by date. Her sassy, sarcastic, sensual approach to life, feels completely contemporary. Set in the clip joints and night clubs of Harlem, Babe's upward nubility takes her from the boxing rings into the celebritocracy of New York and Paris. Babe Gordon is a woman who knows what side her bed is buttered on.

It has been a real pleasure to dive between these covers and discover the real Mae West: not just the unthinking man's Dorothy Parker, and certainly not the prototype for Marilyn Monroe (Mae would never have sung 'Mr President' with such simpering slaveishness).

The only drawback to spending time in Mae West's company is the danger of contracting one-liner-itis. I've been sashaying round with my hand on one hip (not a good look with a baby on the other) rehearsing spontaneous husky-voiced quips for weeks now.

Yet despite her status as a cultural 'come up and see me sometime' icon, she remained down to earth, a self made woman, who didn't worship her creator. Mae West wrote her novels to disprove the accepted notion that, as a woman, it was considered stupid to be too clever. In a man's world, she had what it took to take what they had.

Kathy Lette, London 1995

1

BABE GORDON

BABE GORDON leaned against the crumbling red brick wall of the Marathon Athletic Club in Harlem, at 135th Street off Fifth Avenue, and pulled at a cigarette. The Saturday night fight crowd picked its way under the glaring arc lamp in front of the main entrance like a slow-moving blackbeetle. Babe scanned the humans with an eye to business. Babe was eighteen and a prizefighter's tart, picking up her living on their hard-earned winnings. Her acquaintances numbered trollops, murderers, bootleggers and gambling-den keepers. Two well-modelled bare legs were crossed at the ankles; her waist pressed to the wall rose to voluptuous breasts that almost protruded from the negligible neck of her black dress. Babe waited for Cokey Jenny.

Cokey Jenny had led Babe to her first drink in an apartment speakeasy in Harlem, where a coloured woman sold corn whisky to black and white girls and their gentlemen friends, and coke pedlar and sniffer made their 'connection' in safety. As Babe watched the mob push into the fight enclosure, she wondered what the hell was keeping Cokey. A few months ago they had had a run-in with each other. Jenny wanted Babe to get her 'dope' customers, and when Babe told her she was a louse to peddle dope, Jenny drew a knife on her in Toni's. They had a fight in which Jenny fled into the ladies' toilet and locked the door, but Babe waited till Jenny came out and blacked her eye. They had made it up again. They were useful to each other in keeping up their supply of men. Jenny knew all the sporting roughs who had to have their women and who would spend when their rackets were making money. Jenny knew such men as Eddie Brown, a gangster who specialized in shooting up night clubs that ran in opposition to his boss's interests; she knew Wop Russo, who cooked liquor for most of the Harlem dives; the proprietors of the gin mills; the hangers-on of the gambling dens, who came to see the fights and pick a girl for their Sunday drunk. It was Jenny's dive associations that Babe prospered on.

Babe could pluck a hard-boiled racketeer or gambler for every cent he had on him. They shelled out without her having to ask them. The Harlem magdalens knew she could bring down big money in the high-class hook-shops without having to sit around in dark gutter basements all night guzzling cheap drinks while coaxing some lost sailor into a two-dollar assignation.

Cokey Jenny drew along. A soiled green dress, a flaming red felt hat and dusty satin slippers were the total wardrobe her rambling body carried. She struck a sporty note with a flashy black oilcloth purse. Jenny's gin voice was a scraping rasp. Her eyes resembled steel-headed prison bolts as the cruel purple mouth opened into a witch-laughing salute to Babe. Babe nailed her with a cross-examining eye, and stabbed her with slow words of pain that touched Jenny's pride.

'You walkin' gin house, what the hell's the meanin' of bein' late like this? I had three tumbles the time I've been waitin' for you.'

'What a' ya talkin' about? I ain't touched no gin since last night.'

'Damn liar! Bet you wouldn't be here now, if Toni hadn't pulled the bottle out of your hand and put you out.'

'I was up at Nigger Gert's. A guy up there busted Sing Sing, an' he sent me word he wanted a fix-up of coke with his liquor. Jackass is goin' to pull another job. Look, here's the dough. Five bucks he give me for a couple of powders. I didn't even take a drink from Gert. Who's been blowin' around to-night?'

'Saw Tiger Williams,' said Babe, 'breeze in with the manager of the Black and Tan Revue. I'm not so particular to-night. I'm tellin' you I ain't passin' up anything that looks like a lousy buck. I got to give that landlady somethin' besides a by-and-by smile to-morrow. Ought to be some class, though, in this bunch to-night. Maybe a bank roll.'

A classy dinge passed them by and gave Babe the eye.

'Oh, did you see that?' cried Babe. 'Kinder Spanish lookin'.'

'Do you know him?' asked Jenny.

'Looks like one of them light-coloured musicians at the Bamboo Inn.'

'How about him? Thought you was willin' to make a dollar to-night.'

'Shut up! I tell you, handsome niggers is lookin' for white women to live on. Hell! get some education while you're in Harlem.'

'You must of had that kind.'

'Maybe that's how I know.'

'Sure wish somethin' rotten would turn up now. There's Wop Russo goin' in with a high yella. Sure a classy mulatto jane. I ain't seen him up here for months. Here comes Charlie Yates, and I'll bet he spits right in your eye, too,' Jenny ended.

'Come on,' said Babe. 'Let's look 'em over from inside and do our stuff.'

Babe and Jenny showed their tickets and passed into the packed fight arena. They could solicit here without running the danger they faced on the streets, of being picked up by the cops. The sides of the arena were four black mountain slopes of human life sprinkled with white dots like a stretched curtain. The canvas of the square roped ring glistened white under a dozen overhead X-ray lamps. The restless spectators were howling and stamping for the bouts to begin. Babe and Jenny, among the last to enter, had aisle seats down in front and were instantly recognized by the old-timers of the fight club. Babe gave them all the glad-eye and they hailed back with a chorus of familiar whistling and good-natured guying. They knew that the two molls were there for no good reason; that they had ploughed in all the extraordinary lusts that bestial men, who love prizefighting, subjected their paid women to. As they took their chairs, the girls were bombarded with an avalanche of reek.

'Hello there, Babe! You're lookin' good, kid, even if you don't get out of bed much.'

'Hot shot! Here's the hot-point sisters again!'

The big crowd enjoyed the belt-line comedy. The girls were suddenly the centre of curious attention and the target of wise-cracks.

'Who are the dames?'

'Couple of overtime mammas doin' piece work!'

Babe and Jenny passed through the brute barrage of ridicule with accustomed indifference. All the jeering excited them no more than if ice water ran in their veins. In fact, they liked it. Babe was an amazing contrast to the gawky-limbed, criminal-featured, dumb-minded companion at her side – Cokey Jenny. Jenny was a natural stone in the cesspool of that arena.

Babe calmly looked about and studied the faces. There were half a dozen she recognized as former business acquaintances. There was a face now beaming at her. When had she been with him? Oh yes, Saturday night. He was the fighter that had won a bout last week and spent his winnings on her. His face was healed now. That's why she hadn't immediately recognized him. Babe seldom forgot the faces of her income.

Jenny seemed quiet and drowsy for a short time and Babe knew that this was the result of a pipe of opium she had smoked up at Gert's. Jenny only lived for the dreams she got out of poppy seed. Babe didn't go in for that sort of thing . . . yet. She got too many kicks out of life in other ways. Jenny didn't care for the boys as Babe did. Jenny tolerated men because they went with dope and money. Babe was the type that thrived on men. She needed them. She enjoyed them and had to have them. Without them she was cold and alone. Nature creates different kinds of females and makes them perplexingly contrary to a moral law that assumes all female flesh to be the same. As a matter of fact there are women so constituted that physically and mentally they have no desire for men and therefore become old maids, or enter nunneries. There are women who live a normal, conventional sex life and enter into marriage and motherhood. And then there are women so formed in body and mind that they are predestined to be daughters of joy. These women, whom the French call 'femmes amoureuses', are found not alone among women of the streets, but in every stratum of society. History's pages reveal the power of these women who thrive on love, whose lives are centred on men.

Babe was born a femme amoureuse. Her idea was that if a man can have as many women as he wants, there is no reason why a woman should not do the same thing. She was one of those women who were put on this earth for men – not one man but many men. If a man didn't go for her, she'd wonder what was the matter, she would think she wasn't appreciated. Not that every one who tried for her would succeed, for she did all the picking.

Babe was non-moral. If she had tried to rationalize her attitude, she would have said that the whole world is selling something: goods, ability, personality. Just as a salesman would sell his goods with every ounce of energy and then sit back and enjoy his success, so Babe would enjoy selling herself and

5

her personality. The manner in which she would walk by a crowd of men, or even one man – the toss of her head, the flash of her eye, the light of her smile, all were calculated to win patronage and the consumer's dollar.

Every man she looked at she sized up as a fighter would an opponent. How would she handle him, out-smart him, out-point him? It wasn't hard circumstances – it wasn't a background of disappointment – that made Babe what she was. She was just made for men.

With Jenny, it was a different story. After a disappointing love affair, because of her natural weakness she took to drugs and then the easiest way. She was really not as bad as she was weak. She would have been satisfied with one man but the man she loved she could not have, and this was the easiest way to forget.

The announcer stepped into the ring to introduce the boys for the first bout: a good-looking French light-middleweight and an Italian. Lots of wops fought at the Club, and Babe had tried them a-plenty, but a Frenchman was somewhat of a novelty. She had heard they were unusual in matters of love. They had a superior knowledge of the grand passion, just as educated guys understood algebra where most people were only wise to plain arithmetic. It made her think of that wisecrack, 'Fifty million Frenchmen can't be wrong.' She'd watch this boy. She could get an idea, from the way a fighter handled himself in the ring, of the way he treated women. If he was awkward in fighting, he'd be awkward in love. She'd see what his style suggested. If it promised something different – a new kick – she'd go out for him. Babe always picked her men. She was favourite moll around the Marathon Fight Club, and she chose her boy friends with the care a debutante used in selecting gowns.

The gong sounded. It was a bloody affair of clinches. The fighting was terrific. The Frenchman was flashy and graceful. He was knocked out in the second round. Babe knew she might as well look elsewhere for that night. She nudged Jenny.

'Well, that let's him out as far as I'm concerned.'

Jenny replied without enthusiasm: 'Give me a healthy spaghetti-twister any time.'

'I don't mind a healthy Wop myself, now and then, but I was thinkin' just for a change. You know, if I never made a Frenchman, I'd feel that my education would be sadly neglected.'

The bell sounded again. A Jap and a Catholic boy, who first crossed himself, tore into each other. The Jap pulverized the white boy, and the yellow heads of the Japs at the ringside popped out of the black slopes like blooming dandelions. The mix was stopped before the round was over, the Jap being declared the winner.

Next Alessandro Rosa and Honey Boy Adams, a Cuban black and a Harlem negro, bantam-weights, whipped around the ring like chocolate cake batter. The Cuban scored a win. Clyde Jackson and Spike McCarthy, heavyweights, knocked into each other like rolling beer casks for four rounds to a draw. Walter Erickson and Oscar Peters, lightweights, hung on to each other like two drunks tying to tell each other a story.

'Same old ham card to-night, Jenny,' Babe commented.

'Yeah. Guess it's a gin can for us after the next juggling bout.' She grinned in anticipation. Then, 'Look, Babe.' Jenny pointed to a corner upstairs where a door opened. 'There's Charlie Yates comin' out of the dressin'-room. He's got a new fighter, I hear. What d'ya know about that. Maybe he's breakin' him in here to-night. Sure, he is! There he comes down the stairs!'

Babe turned to Pat Flannigan, a fireman she knew from the 145th Street station house, who knew Charlie Yates well.

'Yates got somethin' on here to-night?'

'The main bout,' Flannigan said. 'Comin' on now.'

'What kind of a socker is he?'

'A middleweight. Charlie says he's the best-looking pug he's ever bumped into. Certainly does look like class, too.'

'You know him?'

'Charlie introduced me to him. I was watching him work out a few times at the 125th Street gym.'

'Where'd Charlie get him?'

'You'd laugh. Picked him off a truck.'

'Oh, a truck-driver. How lovely! I could care for that. What's his name?'

'Bearcat Delaney.'

'Oh yeah?'

'Sure, he's doin' six rounds with Blacksmith Cooper. Ought to be a swell battle.'

Jenny grabbed Babe's arm. 'Charlie's lamped us,' she said.

'Well, that's goin' to spoil his whole evening.' Babe laughed.

'Now don't do no low-crackin' with him. Here he comes.'

Charlie Yates, dapper little manager of several promising white fighters, was turning into the aisle where Babe and Jenny sat, a toothpick stuck in the corner of his mouth and his keen blue eyes snapping confidently out of his thin serious face. Charlie stepped down the aisle toward the ring. Just as he neared Babe, she flung a leg nonchalantly over her knee into his path. Charlie had to sidestep her and his lips twisted into a forced grin.

'Hello, Charlie. What've you got to-night?'

'Nothin' for you,' Charlie cut back at her.

Babe yelled back at him.

'Well, I'll look it over anyway!'

Charlie took a seat at the ringside. Blacksmith Cooper with his seconds climbed through the ropes at the front corner of the ring. He was big-chested and powerfully developed through the shoulders; arms like the legs of a meat block and a cannon-ball head. He was wrapped in a purple padded robe with yellow lapels, his name in yellow letters across the back of the robe. Limbering up on the ropes he resembled a jungle ape. The referee and announcer waited for the other fighter coming down the aisle toward the vacant corner. Bearcat Delaney swung himself easily through the ropes of the upper ring. A cream-coloured bathrobe, left unfastened, revealed the healthy tan of outdoor training, and the firm muscles that moved like oiled springs as he stepped to his corner. His seconds followed him. The crowd looked at this young pugilist with respectful admiration. Handclapping broke out over the arena.

The announcer walked down to the centre of the ring and shot up his hand for silence. Jerking his thumb at the blacksmith in the left corner, he barked:

'Blacksmith Cooper, East Side, weight one hundred and sixty-four,' then jerked his right thumb swiftly at the other corner: 'Bearcat Delaney, Jersey City, weight one hundred and sixty.'

A wide grin broke over the Bearcat's face. The crowd was curious about the newcomer. Shouts went up as the two men met in the centre of the ring and clasped gloves.

'Where'd ya get the Bearcat, Charlie?'

Charlie passed the word that Bearcat was off a truck. It was bait for the crowd.

White silk trunks covered the middle of Bearcat's body. Dark brown wavy hair, smoothed back from a triangle point on his well-shaped forehead, set off a square-jawed face. A medium-sized nose that had been broken emphasized the strength of a well-formed mouth. Grey-green eyes studied everything with a smiling calm. Babe saw instantly that he was something, and then some.

'Who you for?' Jenny asked.

'You'd be surprised,' Babe drawled, and leaned forward. The gong sounded!

'Come on, Blacksmith!'

'Come on, Bearcat! Do your stuff!'

With a cat-like movement, and arms moving like a piston, the Bearcat forged a ring around the solar plexus of the Blacksmith.

'Look at that, Babe. He's got the horseshoe dizzy already. It's goin' to be a knockout. Charlie's got a champ this time sure. Look at him dance and sock.' Babe's eyes sneaked over to Charlie, who was watching his boy with satisfied pride. A great shout rose. The Bearcat had tripped but was fighting back from his knees and laughing and hammering blows all over the Blacksmith as the bell rang for the end of the round. A great roar went up.

'You're all right, Bearcat.'

'Yo' sure can go, white boy!'

'You'd better not step between them headlights, Blacksmith!'

'Watch out. That truck-driver's gonna run you down, Blacksmith!'

Around the slopes, silver and notes flashed out and were staked on the number of rounds the fight would go – what the decision would be. Bets were made that the Bearcat would slip over a K.O. by the third round. Jenny grabbed Babe excitedly. Babe sat in a daze watching the Bearcat smile as the seconds sponged him with water. Jenny rattled on.

'He's goin' to be hard to make, Babe. I told you not to crack with Charlie. You know you ain't got a chance now. And look what we're missin' if this truck-driver lands in the dough. Hell's a matter with you anyway? Don't you hear me?'

'Don't bother me!'

The bell sounded again. Five more rounds to go. Four of them contained sensational fighting with the Bearcat defending himself brilliantly against the veteran blacksmith. The crowd gave the Bearcat a great hand as he finished the fifth round with one more go.

'What an engine that truck has!'

'Cool off his motor there, seconds!'

'Yes, sir, he's steamin' now!'

'Give him those sledgehammers of yours, Blacksmith!'

'What a chassis you got, Bearcat!'

'You should of brought one of your horseshoes along, Blacksmith. You'd sure knock him out.'

'Hit him with that steering-gear, Bearcat!'

'Give him a little oil!'

A little fellow in the balcony arose and recited:

'"Under the spreading chestnut tree, the village smithy stands."'

The crowd howled with glee.

The gong sounded for the last round.

2

THE WINNER

BLACKSMITH COOPER, saving his surprise tactics for the last round, beat upon the body of Bearcat with all his anvil strength. All at once iron sledgehammers seemed to be crushing mercilessly against a white pillar there in the ring. In another minute it would be smashed to pieces.

The crowd sat tense and breathless, watching the pitiless gloves like a hail of shells exploding about the white column that was Bearcat. In another second it would come crashing down. It would be blasted, wiped out by the dynamite charge laid against it.

Then, suddenly, from the ring there came a sound like a loud hand-clap. Babe looked up and saw the Blacksmith go flying against the ropes as if shot from a cannon. In an instant Bearcat was at him, driving vicious rights and lefts into a body that was too hurt to protect itself. Blacksmith sagged; his face turned up hideously contorted, his eyes rolling back till only the whites showed. He slumped to the floor on his face and moved no more till the referee counted him out and Bearcat helped carry him to his corner.

The crowd was delirious with excitement, as the announcer shot his hand to the Bearcat's corner declaring him the winner, by a knockout.

Streaming with perspiration, bruised and happy, the

Bearcat was muffled in his bathrobe and congratulated by his seconds and trainer. Then an enthusiastic delegation of drivers from the American Railway Express Company swept down on him and it took the combined efforts of ringside attendants and police to rescue him from his friends.

'Good boy!' shouted Charlie. 'I knew you'd do it!'

The crowd, curious for a close-up of the Bearcat, was hemmed tightly about the new idol who was making progress back to the dressing-room very slowly. Only after the cops were able to break up the mob did Bearcat get elbow room.

Joe Malone, a fighter who had once made Babe and who occasionally smoked hop with Jenny, was pushing his way to mit the Bearcat, who had finally reached the stair-landing. His mouth was bloody and swollen.

'Swell kid!' Joe Malone shouted.

Bearcat waved. Babe fixed her eyes greedily on him.

'I'll be up in a minute,' Malone called, and turned to look into Babe's eyes.

'Oh, hello, Joe,' she greeted him.

'Well, if it ain't the Babe, and Jen, too,' he said. 'Swell mix, 'at las' one, eh?'

'Not so bad, Joe. What are you rushin' for?'

'Aw, I can't step out witcha to-night, hon.'

'Why not?'

'I'm takin' the Bearcat around to Toni's to eat. Him an' his friends. Ain't he a wow?'

'Yeah, I'll say so!' the Babe exclaimed. 'Do you know him good?'

'Say, didn't he live at me hotel? I'm de one put Charlie wise to him.'

Two cops coming from the stairway and moving the crowd away stopped as they saw Babe and grinned.

Babe tuned seriously to Joe.

'Joe, I want to meet the Bearcat.'

'You won't if Charlie sees you first.'

'Never mind about Charlie. I want to meet him, you hear?'

'All right,' said Joe.

Bill Larson, a friend of Joe's, came up. Babe knew him, too. They greeted one another.

'Are we goin' over to Toni's?' Bill Larson asked Joe.

'Yeah,' said Joe. 'Soon as the Bearcat gets dressed. Listen, you better duck over there a while 'n' grab a couple of tables.'

'Okay,' said Bill.

'I'm goin' with you,' said Babe.

'Well, come along,' said Bill.

Joe hurried to Bearcat's dressing-room. The old-timer who had called Babe a hot-point sister grabbed her by the arm.

'Hello, baby – how about to-night?'

'Listen, airedale,' she said, 'if I want you I'll whistle for you.' She nudged Jenny, indicating a ring on his hand that was worth about fifty dollars. Jenny saw it and walked off with him.

Babe walked out with Bill and headed for Toni's. She knew then that she was sure to meet the Bearcat.

With her escort, Bill Larson, she walked to the corner of 135th Street and Fifth Avenue, and then turned to the left, walking through a block of chop suey fronts, dance halls, and speakeasies, where you bought gin for ten cents and where high-strung society nerves dropped in incognito for their 'shots' of morphine and coke, while bloodstained criminals sat drinking and smoking at the tables in resigned security. In this block they were in Coke Village, below the deadline in deep Harlem.

They came to 134th Street and dropped a short run of steep stairs to Toni's. Toni's was a basement restaurant of red walls stippled with gold and lighted by blue and red bulbs. It was an Italian place and had become popular as a sporting hangout. The food was good. Fighters from the Marathon Club, managers, and other sporting bloods often dropped in.

Bill arranged to reserve two tables for the expected party,

and Babe and he sat down at one of them to wait. She ordered a gin rickey, while Bill chose rye.

A couple of drunken white girls sat over empty gin glasses at a table near by. Babe knew these hustlers. They were guzzlers. They worked the streets till they made enough for a few drinks and then they parked around the Fifth Avenue creep joints, waiting for downtown explorers that needed a 'steer' to dope or wanted to be led to a 'circus' where women resorted to strange practices to gratify morbid curiosity. There was more money in this racket and it was easier. It took energy to be a leg worker, and they were wasted skeletons, bones showing.

Toni's was crowding up. Musicians and chorus girls from the burlesque houses in 125th Street came in to spend the night and morning over cheap gin and a hunk of chicken.

The Bearcat appeared in the doorway with Joe Malone, Harry Flick, another fighter, and three buddies from the express company. They came toward the tables where Babe and Bill were eagerly awaiting the party.

3

BABE MEETS THE BEARCAT

THE BEARCAT was wearing a neat double-breasted dark suit with a faint stripe running through the material, his hair was brushed down and he looked good to Babe, despite a cut in the corner of his mouth and a slight swelling over his right eye.

'Hello,' said Bill. 'Where's Charlie?'

'He's outside phonin',' replied Joe Malone as he shook hands with Babe. His right eye closed in an outrageous wink. He pulled up a chair next to Babe and turned to the Bearcat. 'Sit here, Bearcat.'

The Bearcat looked at Babe and back to Joe.

'Lemme make you acquainted wit' Bearcat Delaney,' Joe said. He wasn't much on ceremony. 'Dis is Babe Gordon, Bearcat.'

'Pleased to meet you,' said Babe.

'Same here,' said the Bearcat. He sat down next to her.

Then he summoned the waiter and ordered drinks for the crowd, taking only a plain ginger ale for himself. Babe ordered a gin rickey. Bearcat asked her how she liked the fight.

'Great!' cried Babe enthusiastically, as though it had been the most sensational thing that ever happened. 'Big boy, you sure can handle your mits.'

'Well,' said the Bearcat, a little bashfully, 'that's my business. I want to be the best in my class. I'm anxious to get to the top.'

'And you sure will, baby,' she said, 'if you keep doing what you done to-night!'

Then her eye fell on the swollen spot over Bearcat's right eye, where the blacksmith had clipped him.

'Oh,' said Babe sympathetically, placing her soft fingers on the bruise. 'Does it hurt?'

'Naw,' said the Bearcat, a thrill passing through him at the touch of her fingers. 'That ain't nothin'.'

From his forehead her hand moved back over his hair and lingered at the back of his neck. Bearcat's heart began to beat a little abnormally. Her lips were not far away from his, and her breath which came gently against his face was fragrant with some elusive perfume. Her lips looked soft and velvety as a rose-petal. He wanted to kiss her then and there.

The other boys felt the same way. But they saw that the Bearcat was interested in her and laid off. They talked about the fight among themselves and praised the Bearcat loudly.

Charlie Yates appeared in the doorway, and when he saw what was going on his lips contracted into a thin line as he approached the combined tables. He knew Babe. Knew her like a book, for she had ruined more than one promising white hope, so when he saw her hand stroking the Bearcat's head he exploded:

'What the hell do you call this?'

Babe looked up and gave him a smile that was innocence itself.

'It's all right, Charlie,' she said. 'I won't hurt him. I only want to feel his muscles.'

The crowd laughed.

Charlie Yates knew that Babe had beaten him to it. She had already got in some of her fine work, but he'd have her framed before she could really get her hooks on Bearcat. By God, he'd fix her! Charlie had seen too many promising fighters succumb to the enervating charms of mercenary tarts to take any chances now.

And Babe needed but a glance at Charlie's eyes to realize that from that moment forward he was her deadliest enemy.

But Charlie hesitated to make a scene. It was a big night for the Bearcat – the boy deserved a little relaxation, and it might be wise not to be too hard on him. There were plenty of managers who would be glad of the chance to pirate Bearcat from him, even though a solid contract bound them together.

'All right,' said Charlie to the Bearcat, 'have your fun. But don't forget you need rest. I'm going to the hotel now. I want to see you there in an hour.'

'Okay, Charlie,' replied the Bearcat, blushing a little, for Babe still stroked the back of his head. He was a bit ashamed in front of Charlie, with his hard, searching eyes. 'I'll see you in an hour.'

Without so much as a courteous good night to the other members of the party, Charlie turned on his heel and walked out.

'I guess Charlie's mad,' said Babe.

'Yeah,' Bearcat grinned, 'but he'll get over it. He don't like girls.'

'Say, I know Charlie,' Babe informed him. 'He likes girls all right, but he don't want his fighters to like girls. You like me all right, don't you?'

'Sure, why not?' Bearcat felt good. Since his win over the blacksmith, he had more confidence in himself than ever before. Now he ordered another round of drinks for the party, but he himself stuck to ginger ale.

Babe began to feel her liquor a little. She had certain ideas. She wanted to get rid of the others and talk to Bearcat alone. Always resourceful, she quickly found a way.

'Charlie says he wants to see you in an hour,' Babe warned the Bearcat. 'We'd better get started. You can drop me off downtown.'

Babe's suggestion suited Bearcat. He felt an urge to see Babe alone. He did not know much about women, and she held a strange fascination for him.

However, he insisted they all have some food before they left. They ate and drank and talked, and Bearcat paid the bill.

Once outside, Bearcat obtained a cab. He put Babe inside, and climbed in after her. But Joe Malone and two of the boys from the express company said they were going their way and insisted on a ride. This was unlooked for, and Bearcat was peeved, while Babe was furious. She was smouldering inside until the cab arrived at 80th Street, where two of the excess pieces of baggage got out.

'You're sure one swell scrapper, Bearcat,' one of them said. 'We'll tell the boys down at the garage what they missed. Good night, take care of yourself, old-timer.'

Babe was relieved when they had gone. But Joe Malone still remained with them. Every block or two Babe asked him if this was not where he got off. Joe refused to take the hint and grinned maliciously, until at last Columbus Circle hove in sight. There Joe put his hand on the door and said:

'T'anks for a very nice evenin'.' Then he turned to the driver. 'Hey, Mac, let me out here.' The cab jolted to a stop and Joe alighted. With a 'So long!' and a wave of his hand he was gone. The cab continued across the Circle and down Eighth Avenue. There was not a sound for a long time in the back of the cab.

At last Babe and the Bearcat were alone. It was precisely what they had waited for since the moment they had set eyes on each other. Babe finally broke the silence. If the Bearcat had done all the leading in to-night's fight, it was Babe who did all the leading in the cab.

'I thought they'd never go,' said Babe, edging closer to the Bearcat.

'Me either,' said the Bearcat.

'You know,' Babe said, warming up, 'when I saw you in the

ring to-night, I could hardly wait to meet you. Then when I did meet you, I could hardly wait till we were alone.'

'Gee, yeah?' Bearcat experienced a sensation he at first could not account for. Without his quite being conscious of it, she had first taken his hand and then slipped it behind her so that now his left arm encircled her waist. The soft feel of her body against his arm stirred him – because Bearcat was not a ladies' man in the strict sense of the term.

'Well,' Bearcat continued, ''sfunny, but I felt the same way about you, the minute I saw you. When I saw you, I – I thought – there's the prettiest girl I ever seen. An' I wanted to meet you. But I didn't know whether you were with Bill or not.'

'Oh no, I just came over with him. I knew I was goin' to meet you.'

'Uh-huh, I see,' said Bearcat. 'I'm glad.'

'You think I'm pretty?' asked Babe, her eyes widening into his.

'Sure. I'll say I do.'

Babe's head leaned back against his left shoulder. Her lips were only a couple of inches from his when he looked at her. Fate took a hand at that instant. The driver swerved the cab to avoid another car, and the lips of his passengers had a collision. It was a collision that lasted for a long while. It happened at 54th Street and continued to 14th Street, when Babe and the Bearcat came to with a jerk.

Babe laughed.

'Look where we are!'

Bearcat looked and shouted to the driver.

'Hey, buddy, we went too far.' He was referring of course to the distance, not to what had taken place in the back of the cab. 'Turn around and go back to 48th Street. That's where you want to go, ain't it – Babe?'

'Yes,' said Babe with a hidden smile, for it was the first time since they met that he had called her Babe.

However, once started, Bearcat was not the man to stop. So there were more delicious kisses on the way back uptown.

The little cut in the corner of Bearcat's mouth hurt somewhat when they pressed their lips together. But when Babe touched it tenderly and told him she would kiss him on the other corner of his mouth, Bearcat denied that it hurt. He began to feel reckless. He had forgotten about meeting Charlie. His whole desire was to see as much of Babe as possible.

He paused in the midst of caresses to say:

'Babe – can't I see you to-morrow? Can't I take you out to dinner?'

'Yes,' Babe consented; 'but what'll Charlie say?'

Suddenly the idea of Charlie always telling him what to do, and what not to do, seemed burdensome.

'Never mind Charlie,' Bearcat replied. 'I guess I can do what I like.'

'Of course you can,' said Babe. 'Charlie's a good manager and all. But don't let him boss you around. You know you're a good fighter. You'd be a good fighter if Charlie wasn't your manager. So don't let him get too stuck on himself. He'll start thinking he's bigger than you.'

'Sure, you're right about that,' Bearcat agreed.

'Oh, I know Charlie,' said Babe. 'You better not let him know that we're going to see each other. It'll make it uncomfortable for you.'

Bearcat's subconscious yearning for women was having its effect.

'Well, I guess I can go out with you, if I want to. I'm gonna tell him so.'

The cab pulled up at 48th Street. Bearcat paid the driver and dismissed him. Babe lived in a quiet rooming-house in West 48th Street off Eighth Avenue. They stood in the hallway and Babe clung to Bearcat in a good-night kiss.

As they parted, she said:

'Don't say anything to Charlie, about us. It won't do no good.'

'There's no use in sneakin' about it,' said Bearcat. 'I guess I can do what I like. Charlie don't own me. I'll tell him.'

'No, no!' Babe cried quickly. 'He'll only make trouble and separate us. He'll tell you lies about me. Say I'm no good and all that. Maybe he'll get you to believe him.'

'Believe anything he'd say about you?' Bearcat's head went back in surprise. 'I should say not. I'm no fool!'

'Well, promise me you won't say anything to Charlie.'

'All right, if you say so. But don't forget about to-morrow night. I'll meet you on the corner here at six o'clock. Is that okay?'

'That'll be fine, honey,' Babe answered, giving him another long kiss. Then she went upstairs. Bearcat stood looking after her a minute, then he went out into the street and walked on air to his hotel.

Up to now Bearcat really had had no time for women. He had been too concerned with his career as a fighter. A fighter could not mess around with women and expect to arrive anywhere. But to-night the most beautiful woman in the world, to him, had opened the gates to an enchanting though dangerous paradise.

The Bearcat crossed to Broadway and strolled up 54th Street, to the Nelson Hotel, where he had a room. Charlie also lived there. It was an hotel where many fighters found it convenient to stop.

When Bearcat entered he found Charlie and a number of boys waiting up for him. The boys crowded around shaking hands and congratulating him on success.

'Great kid!' they told him with slaps on the back.

'Good stuff, Bearcat. Always knew you couldn't miss!'

'You took him pah-lenty, an' you'll take the rest of 'em, too, sure as hell.'

Charlie greeted him with a sour look. He was sore because the Bearcat had kept him and the boys waiting around.

'Thought you was comin' back in an hour,' growled Charlie. 'Hell of a long hour!'

For the first time the Bearcat felt like coming back at Charlie. He was more annoyed than ever before at Charlie's criticism.

'Had some personal business to 'tend to,' snapped Bearcat, and he turned away to speak to one of the boys. He had as much as told Charlie to mind his own business.

Charlie gave Bearcat a sharp look, and then thought: 'He must be tired, I shouldn't ride him too much.'

Charlie Yates knew the Bearcat inside and out, or up until to-night he had. Every good manager who wishes to make his fighter a winner has got to know the mind as well as the body of his man. A fighter is like a valuable thoroughbred horse, and like one, has to be stabled, fed, and clothed. That's a manager's job.

Charlie Yates had seen the possibilities in Bearcat when the latter was just the rawest of raw material, and it was he who had shaped that raw material into the clever, hard-hitting fighter that Bearcat had shown himself to be that night. When the Bearcat was working his way up, drawing money hardly worth mentioning, it was Charlie who had laid out his own cash to feed, clothe, house and pay for the training of Bearcat. And now he was ready to go through hell and a meat-chopper to prevent Bearcat from ruining his career.

Women are, were, and always will be the fly in the ointment of every fighter who gives them more than a second's thought.

Charlie was too shrewd a fellow to allow the joys of the flesh to come between Bearcat and the triumph of championship. For Charlie saw in Bearcat the man to wear the title, and that within a very short time.

4

BABE WORKS HER POINTS

THE BEARCAT accepted the enthusiastic adulation of the boys in the hotel almost with indifference. His mind was on Babe. The remembrance of her kisses was too fresh and the experience too unusual for him to take the matter casually as another man better versed in the ways of woman might have done.

Charlie lit a long cigar and wandered over to the registration desk to chat with the room clerk.

The buzzer on the switchboard signalling an incoming call sounded, and Barney, a young negro who always wore an expansive grin and at this late hour doubled as lift and switchboard operator, answered the call. His grin became wider as he turned to the clerk.

'Dey's a fair voice on de phone askin' fo' Mistuh Delaney. Yas suh, a berry sweet voice.'

'Shut up, you!' snapped Charlie, in a half-whisper, and threw a glance over his shoulder at the Bearcat. 'Gimme that call.'

'Aw right,' Barney assented with a chuckle.

Charlie stepped quickly to a house phone and lifted the receiver.

'Hello,' he snarled into the mouthpiece. 'Who do you want? Who are you?'

Babe, who was on the other end, immediately recognised Charlie's gruff voice. She was too fast for Charlie.

'Hello, Bearcat,' she said. 'I just wanted to say good night, dear. Get a good rest, honey.'

Charlie banged down the receiver. His teeth clamped his cigar like a vice. He went back to the desk and leaned over toward the clerk.

'Listen, Jack,' he said, 'if any dames call up for the Bearcat, switch 'em on to me. Get me?'

'That's okay with me,' replied the clerk. 'You know what you're doing.'

'You're damn right I do,' said Charlie, puffing furiously at his cigar. 'All that guy needs is a few dames an' he's through.'

'Oh, sure, they're bad stuff,' said the clerk – 'for a fighter,' he added qualifyingly.

Charlie walked over and took Bearcat by the arm.

'You've been up late enough, kid. Come on to bed.'

Bearcat was tired and glad to get away from the admiring crowd. But he set himself for a laying out from Charlie, and he was surprised when the latter left him at the door to his room, with a brief 'Good night.'

The Bearcat proceeded to undress rapidly. To-morrow was Sunday, and he was glad he could spend the day loafing. He thought of his coming date with Babe, and sat on the edge of the bed with one sock in his hand, while he grieved over his neglect in not inquiring if Babe had a telephone.

'Now, there is one swell girl,' he thought, as he exercised for fifteen minutes. 'The kind of a girl who could help a fellow. With a girl like that back of him, a guy could be a real success.'

After a shower he jumped into bed and soon was asleep, his last fleeting thoughts being about Babe and their meeting to-morrow.

In the morning, he was up and dressed by eleven o'clock. He hated to think that he would have to wait nearly seven whole hours before he would see Babe. He breakfasted lightly in the hotel and strolled into the lobby to kill some time.

Charlie was sitting comfortably in one of the deep leather chairs with a half-smoked cigar tilted at right angles in his mouth.

'Have a good sleep?' he asked.

'Sure,' replied the Bearcat. 'I feel great.'

'You got some great write-ups in the papers,' Charlie said. 'They all say you look like champeenship material. See, ain't that what I been tellin' you right along?'

'Yeah,' said the Bearcat. 'Well, you know I'm achin' to be the champ, Charlie.'

'An' if I got anything to do with it, you will be,' answered Charlie, tossing his cigar-butt into a convenient cuspidor. He looked up into Bearcat's face searchingly.

Bearcat felt a wave of uneasiness sweep over him. He knew Charlie was suspicious of his actions the night before. He felt guilty, but he resented Charlie's suspicion, the more so because Charlie was right.

'Nice day,' the Bearcat murmured.

'Perfect,' said Charlie. 'How about goin' for a auto ride this afternoon? We can drive up through Westchester, have dinner on the way back, and you can hit the hay early. You got to get down to the gym early Monday morning.'

This suggestion did not suit Bearcat at all. Another time he would have welcomed it. But now, if he went riding with Charlie, he would not be able to keep his appointment with Babe.

The day clerk stuck his head around the corner of the cashier's cage and called.

'Telephone for Mr. Delaney.'

The Bearcat went briskly to an extension.

Charlie wondered who it could be. He hoped it was not Babe. He had failed to warn the day clerk to switch to him all calls from women intended for the Bearcat.

'Hello,' said the Bearcat.

The rich, alluring voice of Babe Gordon came to his ear.

'Hello, honey,' said Babe. 'How are you this morning?'

The Bearcat lowered his voice.

'Babe, I'm glad you called up.'

'Are you, dear?' asked Babe. 'Well, I just got back from church, and I thought I'd give you a ring.'

If Babe had gone to church, and just got back, she certainly must have attracted a lot of attention from the congregation, for as she now stood talking over the pay telephone in the hall of her rooming-house, she wore a pink dressing-gown and underneath it the sheerest of step-ins which would have popped the eyes out of the most near-sighted of deacons.

'Church?' queried the Bearcat, mildly surprised. 'Well, you're better than me. I didn't go at all. I just about got out of bed. But as long as you go for both of us, I guess its all right.'

'Oh, I said a prayer for you,' lied Babe. 'Honey, it's almost twelve o'clock. Couldn't I meet you at one and have dinner with you, instead of waiting until to-night?'

'Well, I'd sure like to,' said the Bearcat earnestly. 'But Charlie wants me to go ridin' with him up to Westchester or some place. I don't want to go, but how can I get out of it, without gettin' him sore?'

Babe thought quickly.

'If you went with him you wouldn't get back to meet me to-night. So why not meet me on my corner in a half-hour? Then after we eat you can go ridin' with Charlie. There's no use in startin' trouble with him now.'

'All right,' the Bearcat agreed. 'Maybe that'll be the best for to-day anyhow. I'll meet you in a half-hour at your corner.'

'Good-bye, baby,' said Babe. 'Don't keep me waitin'.'

'Don't worry, I won't.'

'Good-bye,' said Babe again.

'Good-bye,' said the Bearcat.

He turned away from the phone to find Charlie standing only a foot or two away from him, his hands on his hips.

'Well,' said Charlie, his jaw setting hard, 'who 'n hell was that? A woman, I know. I could hear her squawkin' from over here.'

The Bearcat looked at Charlie uncertainly for an instant. Then he decided he might as well tell him the truth.

'It was Babe,' the Bearcat confided.

'Come over here,' said Charlie; he walked over to where two chairs were close together. 'Sit down.'

The Bearcat lowered himself into a chair and threw a leg over one of its arms.

Charlie sat down and bit into a fresh cigar. Then he slid forward on the end of his chair and leaned his face close to the Bearcat. His voice was low but firm.

'What do you think you're doin'?' he inquired coldly.

'I ain't doin' nothin',' said the Bearcat. 'There ain't no harm in takin' a girl to dinner, is there?'

'Takin' what girl to dinner? Babe?'

'Sure.'

Charlie's lip curled.

'You might as well be takin' a load of dynamite to dinner and start kickin' it around.'

'Don't talk foolish, Charlie. I'm tellin' you, Babe's all right. She's different.'

'You're goddam right she's different!'

'Why, only just now,' the Bearcat went on, 'she told me she came from church.'

'What?' Charlie shouted. He lost his balance on the edge of the chair and hit the tiled floor with a bump. The shock had been too much for him.

The Bearcat sprang up with a look of concern.

'What's the matter!' he cried, as he lifted Charlie to his feet. 'Are you hurt?'

Charlie was shaking with laughter. 'Church!' he yelled,

going off into another gale of laughter. Bearcat had never seen him laugh like that before.

The manager sank weakly into his chair.

'I ain't had a belly-laugh like that in a year,' he said. Then he looked sad, as he discovered that in falling he had ruined a perfectly good cigar.

His head went up and his eyes flashed angrily.

'Don't be a sap! Babe Gordon go to church! Why the place'd cave in on her. If you said she went to hell, I'd believe you.'

The Bearcat's face was a dangerous red.

'Well, whether you believe it or not, I'm leavin' now to have dinner with her. If you want to go ridin' I'll be back here at two o'clock. If you don't, say so now.'

Then they stared at one another in silence for what seemed a long while.

Charlie broke the stillness.

'I can see where life is gonna be hell from now on.' He rose and walked straight to the lift which took him aloft.

The Bearcat turned and went out of the hotel, walking rapidly toward Eighth Avenue.

When Babe Gordon had told the Bearcat she had been to church, it never occurred to her that she was lying. That is, it had no moral significance for her. To Babe, a lie was simply something one told to gain an advantage, to get what one wanted by the shortest route. She never lied just for the sake of lying. When she had lied she had a definite reason for doing so. It was for the purpose of creating a valuable impression. Charlie might say things about her, which, even if Bearcat did not believe them outright, might cause him to have suspicions. Therefore, she had made up the story about going to church. Bearcat was now convinced that she was a good girl, had character; and now, no matter what Charlie said against her, if she were careful Bearcat would always believe in her.

Babe was the living example of all that is immoral, when viewed through conventional eyes. But she herself was unmoral. For her, morals did not exist. She would not have known what a moral was if it could be made to dance naked in front of her.

As she prepared her toilette before going to meet the Bearcat, she looked at her glowing body with self-appreciation. The well-turned arms and legs, the smooth contour of curving hips, her pink, curling toes, all combined to give her a thrill of sensuous pleasure and to remind her how she might captivate any man.

'How nice I am,' she thought, as she enumerated to herself all the points of her alluring perfection.

Babe attired herself with particular care, and when at the appointed time she met the Bearcat on the corner she certainly made a ravishing appearance.

'You sure look good to me,' the Bearcat commented.

'You don't look so bad yourself,' said Babe, with a gracious smile.

'Are you hungry?' asked the Bearcat.

'Well,' Babe responded, 'I could do dirt to a good meal. How about you?'

'Oh, I always got a good appetite,' the Bearcat answered.

'There's a nice place on 48th Street, over near Sixth Avenue,' Babe told him.

'Anything you say's all right with me,' the Bearcat said smilingly.

They walked toward Broadway, Babe tucking her right arm under the Bearcat's brawny left.

The place was an Italian restaurant, dimly lighted with little lamps at each table. They had a *table d'hôte* dinner for a dollar and a half, which Babe ordered. The Bearcat was undecided at first, whether he wanted that much to eat, since he had had a late breakfast, but he saw nothing to his liking that was not included in the dinner, so he also chose the *table d'hôte*. The heavy, greasy food was certainly not the kind for a fighter in training and the Bearcat had his doubts whether he should touch any of it. However, Babe tasted the thick *minestrone* soup and pronounced it good, and the Bearcat feeling embarrassed at his hesitation, waded into the food and ate everything in sight.

Babe's appetites were always lusty and it was not till she had finished two large helpings of soup that she felt any desire to talk.

The first thing she said was:

'Honey, the more I see you the more I like you.'

'You ain't kiddin' me, are you?' the Bearcat asked earnestly.

'You know I'm not. I like you better than any fellow I ever met.'

The Bearcat lowered his voice.

'Babe,' he said, 'I don't know much about girls. I suppose you think I'm a dumb guy. But I like you a lot.'

'I don't think you're dumb at all,' Babe rested her hand lightly on his huge paw. 'No dumb guy could fight like you do.'

The Bearcat leaned forward in his chair.

'I'd like to take you out all the time, Babe,' he said. 'But I want you to be my girl. I mean' – he was confused – 'if you like me as much as you say, I don't want you to bother with no other guys.'

Babe hesitated a moment.

'All right, honey,' she said then, 'I won't look at another fellow. But I got to see you every day then. I get lonesome, and I don't want to hang around a roomin'-house alone every night.'

'Don't worry about that,' the Bearcat said, slipping his hand over hers. 'We'll have a good time together. I don't mean for you to be lonesome.'

When the Bearcat had left her to keep his appointment with Charlie, Babe walked along Broadway for a block or two. She smiled confidently to herself. She had got her man – got him in the palm of her hand. But while she felt a distinct pleasure in the knowledge, she was forced to admit that she had a deeper, more genuine, liking for this simple, boyish fellow than that which had first motivated her when she had schemed to meet him the night of the fight. Calculatingly, she meant to make the companionship a profitable one for herself, but at the same time she planned to give the Bearcat his money's worth in pleasure.

She turned into a drug store and from a phone booth called Cokey Jenny, and arranged to see a motion picture with her. Babe longed for the gorgeous trappings of romance that she saw pictured on the silver screen, and she dreamed that some day all the pleasure and refinements of luxury would be hers. She saw herself the adored mistress of a handsome, aristocratic young god who possessed all the wealth of Crœsus.

5

THE MODEL

THAT night Babe went to bed early for the first time
for months. She had come to a decision. For a short
period she had been a model for Goldstein, in his
gown shop in West 36th Street. She had been Goldie's star
model, and when she had left him to seek an easier life in the
dusk-till-dawn existence of Harlem, he had mourned her loss.

Now she wanted to play safe. She meant to concentrate
on holding the Bearcat, who she thought would soon be
champion, and as such would command large slices of heavy
gate receipts. To be on the safe side, she would chuck Harlem
and drinking and late hours and men, so that neither Charlie
nor the Bearcat could point a finger at her. She decided to
go back to work for Goldstein. It meant getting to the shop
at ten o'clock every morning. But she would be drawing a
regular salary, could dress better, and move to more attractive
quarters. Besides, having a job would give her, in the Bearcat's
eyes, the appearance of respectability, which that unsophis-
ticated young man thought essential in a girl – that is, his own
particular girl.

At nine o'clock Monday morning Babe entered Goldstein's
establishment. She went into his private office without
knocking. Goldie looked up from his desk and stared. Then
he threw up his hands.

'Good God! Babe!' he cried, in genuine astonishment.

'Hello, Goldie,' she said with a winsome smile.

He came around his desk and pumped her arm up and down. He seemed tickled to see her. He had always held a soft spot in his heart for her.

'Dis is a surprise,' he said, his fat face beaming. 'So what are you doing now?'

'Nothing,' Babe replied. 'Nothing at all. And I'm tired of doing it. Thought I'd drop in and see if you had any models I could buy cheap.'

'Sure, sure,' said Goldie. 'We got plenty, and a new line we just made up. Come, I show you.'

They went into the salesroom and Goldie showed her all sorts of smart models in suits and dresses. She tried on one of the latest in dresses and Goldie raved over her.

'Perfect!' he shouted, as he always did when he was excited. 'You were made for it – I mean it was made for you. Such a model, oy!' An idea struck him. 'Listen, Babe, listen! Vy you don't come back to work for me? Look, you could get yourself some nice clothes reasonable. Understand? Look, I'll pay you twenty-five dollars a week.'

Babe knew she had him going.

'Well I don't know, Goldie,' she said slowly. 'Twenty-five ain't much and —'

'I'll make it thirty, for you, Babe. Thirty dollars, understand? For nobody else I vouldn't do it.'

Babe knew that was his limit. He wouldn't go higher for Gloria Swanson.

'All right,' said Babe. 'Thirty it is.'

Goldie snatched up her hand and led the way back to his private office.

'I knew you vould do it for Goldie,' he said. 'And besides, listen – the buyers vill be comin' in town next veek. Babe, you vill make yourself a lot of *gelt*, understand? And look, what nice garments you can get here. You like nice things,

Babe, I know you. You do right by Goldie and he does right by you!'

'What do you mean?' asked Babe with a laugh. 'That sounds like a proposition.'

'Ah, Babe, you know what I mean,' he said reproachfully. 'I only mean you good. You vouldn't vant a old feller like me.'

'You never can tell,' laughed Babe. 'You might have some fireworks left.'

'Vell,' said Goldie with a grin, 'maybe a couple of sky-rockets yet.'

They both laughed. They understood each other, those two. He admired Babe because she could get the best of him, even more than for her beauty.

At noon, Babe called up the Bearcat at his hotel. He was waiting around hoping she would call, as she had promised.

'I'm working,' she told him, 'and I got till one o'clock for lunch. I'd like to have it with you, if you can come right down.'

'You bet I can,' said the Bearcat eagerly.

'Well, meet me in front of 200 West 36th Street, honey, as soon as you can.'

'I'll be right down,' said the Bearcat. 'I'll grab a cab.'

He hung up and almost ran into the street, where he hailed a cab and jumped in.

Babe turned from the phone and ran her eye over the lines and lines of models hanging on racks. She could use a couple of them, she thought. Then she put on her hat and went out to the lift.

'I didn't know you was workin',' said the Bearcat, as he faced Babe across the luncheon-table.

'Well, I am, you see,' she said. 'I'm a model, and Goldstein, that's the guy I work for, says I'm one of the best in the business.'

'You ain't one of these here artist models?' the Bearcat asked suspiciously.

Babe laughed.

'No. But I guess I could be one of them, if I wanted to. I got the shape and everything.'

'Well,' said the Bearcat, 'I hope you won't do nothin' like that.'

'Don't worry, honey,' the Babe said, her eyes flattering him with their glance. 'I'll stick to suits and dresses.'

The Bearcat breathed a sigh of relief.

'Oh, suits and dresses. Well, I bet you look swell in 'em.'

'Well, I ought to,' said Babe as she attacked her soup. 'Goldie sure has some pretty dresses. You know, I can pick up a lot of dresses cheap from Goldie.'

'Yeah?' said the Bearcat. 'Gee, I guess you're lucky. A lot of girls would like to be in your shoes, hey?'

Babe pushed her plate to one side and watched the Bearcat as he shovelled in the soup.

'You know, I can buy dresses from Goldie for fifty dollars each. Dresses that retail at a hundred each.'

'Say, that's a bargain, ain't it?' The Bearcat wiped his mouth with a napkin and leaned back in his chair.

'Sure,' said Babe. 'I'm tryin' to save a little money and get a couple of new dresses. I need 'em. Besides, I want to look nice when I go out with you.'

'You always look good to me, Babe,' said the Bearcat fervently.

Babe had an idea.

'I wish you'd come up to the place and help me pick out a couple of dresses,' she said. 'I know Goldie'll let me pay for them out of my salary, so much a week. You'll come up, won't you? I want to be sure and get something you like.'

'Well, I don't know,' the Bearcat said. 'I don't know much about women's clothes, Babe. Anything you pick out will look good to me, as long as you're wearin' it.'

'Oh, come up anyway,' said Babe. 'I want to show you all

those nice new dresses. Besides, we've got some nice models workin' there.' She gave the Bearcat a sly glance.

'I ain't interested in no other girl but you,' said the Bearcat sincerely.

'All right, then. Just come up to please me.'

'Well, I'd like to, Babe. But gee, I'd feel foolish in a woman's dress place. Look,' he added, and his right hand slid into his pocket, 'anything you pick out will be just fine.'

He brought out an immense roll of bills. He had received seven hundred dollars as his share of Saturday night's battle. He had almost five hundred left after Charlie Yates' share had been deducted.

'Gosh!' said Babe. 'You carryin' all that money around with you?'

'Sure,' said the Bearcat with a grin, 'why not?' He stripped two one hundred dollar bills off the roll, leaned forward and laid them next to Babe's plate. 'There – get yourself a couple of nice dresses.'

'Oh!' exclaimed Babe, in feigned astonishment. 'Why, Bearcat! I can't take that.' Her hand folded over the bills.

'Sure, you can,' said the Bearcat. 'It's just a little present from me.'

'But you oughtn't to do it,' Babe said, making the bills disappear into her purse.

'Now don't say nothin' more about it,' the Bearcat ordered. 'I want you to look good when you're with me.'

'Well, honey,' said Babe. 'You're one great pal.'

The Bearcat blushed.

'Of course,' he said, 'I don't want you to wear them dresses if you go out with other guys.'

'I ain't goin' out with other guys,' Babe assured him. 'Nobody but you, honey.'

'You mean that?'

'I wouldn't lie to *you*, dear,' said Babe, with rounded eyes that seemed to be speaking the truth.

'All right,' said the Bearcat. 'Oh, I forgot to tell you, Babe, that I'm leavin' for Buffalo to-night. I got a scrap on there next Tuesday night, an' I got to do a lot of trainin' up there beforehand.'

'Oh,' said Babe. 'I'll be awful lonesome while you're away, dear, but you don't need to fret, I won't bother with no other fellows. I might go to the pictures or a show with Jenny, but that's all.'

'If I win this fight – an' I know I will – I'll make a sweet little pile.'

'I'll be rootin' for you, honey. Even if I'm not there,' said Babe.

The Bearcat escorted Babe back to Goldstein's and in the hallway of the building, when there was no one about, she gave him a warm kiss. Then, assuring her he would write to her while he was away, he went out.

Babe looked in her purse to be certain that the two hundred dollars was still there. Then she went up in the lift, a contented smile on her face.

6

BABE AND CHARLIE

URING the week that the Bearcat was in Buffalo, Babe received a letter from him every day. The notes were brief, and clumsily written, and while they could hardly have been called love letters, yet their general tone conveyed something of the Bearcat's feeling for Babe. She herself wrote him one letter in which she offered him encouragement in his coming fight in the up-state city, and assured him she was being true to him. She had been careful in composing the letter, for she was shrewd enough to foresee that it might by chance fall under the eyes of Charlie Yates, and she had no intention of his getting anything on her in writing.

Babe was busy, too, during the period of the Bearcat's absence. The buyers were in town and she permitted herself to be taken to theatres and night clubs by them and enjoyed herself thoroughly. However, she allowed them no undue intimacy with her, beyond a few kisses, and for the pleasure of her company the buyers were glad to reward her with various sums of money before they left town. She had brought Goldstein a great deal of business and he was grateful. Her financial condition had so improved that she moved to the Hotel Europe in 49th Street, two days before the Bearcat came home. With the Bearcat's two hundred she had replenished her wardrobe, and she now began to feel almost prosperous.

When the Bearcat came home, the winner of the Buffalo fight and the richer by thirty-five hundred dollars, Babe saw him every day. They went to the pictures, to dinner; and Babe went up to see the Bearcat at the gym when he tipped her off that Charlie would not be present.

But Charlie was not a manager who could be kept in the dark long about what his fighter was up to outside of training hours. He watched every movement of the Bearcat without the fighter knowing that his manager was mentally shadowing him.

At breakfast, over their ham and eggs, Charlie could tell by the brisk way the Bearcat dug into his food and the happy tone of his conversation that he had seen Babe Gordon. At supper when the Bearcat was silent and preoccupied and hurried his food, Charlie knew that he had an appointment with Babe for the pictures. He knew by the shoe-shine, the freshly pressed suit, the favourite necktie, two hair-trims a week instead of one, the increasing intensity of Bearcat's interest in this tart – an interest that would ultimately ruin him. Charlie was too shrewd to read the riot act to Bearcat on the eve of the fight in which he was to meet Harlem Joe Hastings. He knew the importance of the morale that time and again had won victory, when the body seemed doomed to defeat.

He knew that Babe was coming up to the gym the days he was downtown, and Charlie was determined to break up the affair, but he must wait for the right moment. He arranged with the girl at the switchboard of the hotel to tell him all the appointments Bearcat made with Babe.

It was a week before the fight. Charlie and Bearcat had returned from eating. Charlie met some theatrical friends in the lobby and stopped to chat with them. The Bearcat went upstairs, to stretch out, he said. As the lift was taking Bearcat up, Charlie stepped to the desk and wrote something on a sheet of stationery which he asked the clerk to hand over to the telephone girl. Then he rejoined his friends. They were a song and dance team that Charlie had known from his home town. They were just back from the coast. They had been talking Hollywood for an hour when Bearcat stepped out of the lift in a different suit and a new tie. Charlie had purposely seated himself with his back to the lift and desk.

The Bearcat went out of the door without having seen Charlie. Charlie rose and went to the desk. The telephone girl handed him a slip of paper. Charlie glanced at it, looked at his watch, threw his cigar into a cuspidor and started for the Hotel Europe in 49th Street.

He studied the lobby of that hotel, went to the desk and said he wanted to call Miss Gordon's room. The clerk gave him the room number. Instead of phoning, he walked up the stairs to the fifth floor and stopped before room 525. He tapped lightly on the door.

'Who is it?' It was Babe's voice.

'Telegram,' Charlie said.

Babe opened the door. The outlines of her rounded body were revealed through an expensive Fifth Avenue négligé. She met Charlie's eyes with a cool defensive smile.

'So you're a messenger boy now, Mr. Yates. You ain't bringin' bad news, I hope.'

'That depends on you,' said Charlie, walking to the centre of the room, his eyes taking in every detail of the place.

Babe closed the door and locked it; she knew that sooner or later some kind of a show-down must be faced with Charlie. She was ready to call his bluff now.

'Well,' she said, 'get it off your chest.'

He nodded his head toward two handsome gowns and an exclusive-looking hat that were laid out on the bed.

'I suppose you got that junk with Bearcat's dough.'

'I didn't say so,' Babe said sharply.

'You don't have to say anythin', I'll do the talkin'. I know what you're up to. And lemme tell you, sister, you're gonna lay off the Bearcat from to-night on.'

Babe laughed.

'Says you, Mr. Yates.'

'Don't try to be funny,' Charlie growled. His face flushed with anger and he spoke rapidly from the corner of his mouth. 'Listen, you goddam three-dollar tramp, if you think I'm gonna let you make a palooka out of one of the best fighters that ever lived, you're plain nuts. You're quittin' the Bearcat to-night, get me?'

Babe's eyes narrowed. 'Say, you —'

'Shut up!' Charlie barked out. 'You're just a lousy tart peddlin' your stuff to any guy that's got coffee and cake money in his pants. You ain't gonna ruin the Bearcat an' me too, if I have to frame you with the cops. An' I can do it too. If you don't lay off, I'll use every trick I know to railroad you to gaol. I'll get you picked up for hustling, I'll plant dope on you an' tip off the cops so's you'll get three years in stir!'

Suddenly Babe gave a shrill laugh.

'Why, you goddam, low-down, ten-cent bum!' she cried, her eyes turning to flames of fury. 'Think you can threaten me? Turn me in to the cops? Why, I know every cop from here to Harlem, and they'd do more for me for a smile than they'd do for you for all the money you could give 'em!'

Charlie was startled by her onslaught. He had expected her to cower under his threats, but instead she was furiously lashing out at him.

'You got a hell of a nerve comin' up here and insultin' me, and then expecting me to do you a favour and give up the Bearcat.'

'I ain't askin' any favours, I'm tellin' you what you got to do.'

'Did you think I'd fall for your cheap squawking? Take off your hat, goddam you! You ain't even got enough etiquette to take it off in the presence of a lady. Take it off, I said, before I knock it off.'

Charlie was so taken aback, that he quickly removed his hat and sank into a near-by armchair.

'If you'd have come up here in a decent way,' Babe continued, 'and asked me in a nice manner to quit goin' with the Bearcat, I might 'a' thought it over. Now I say no. The idea of a guy, as punk as you, comin' to me with threats and insults, wanting me to give up a guy I really like.'

Charlie thought rapidly. He saw there was nothing to be gained by his former attitude so he tried another approach.

'You mean you really care about the Bearcat?' he asked in a quieter tone.

'That's what I said, and I mean it,' Babe replied. 'He's too damn good a guy to be hangin' on to a louse like you.'

'Wait a minute, Babe. I got the Bearcat's best interest at heart. I don't ask you to do anythin' for me. But if you think anythin' of the Bearcat, you'll leave him alone, till after this fight with Harlem Joe.' He squeezed two tears into the corners of his eyes. 'Babe, don't you understand? Don't you realize what this means to me? Here I have been spending my time and money for years on the Bearcat to make him the fighter he is now. For God's sake, don't ruin him on me. If you want dough – if you need money, I'll give it to you, but please, please gimme a chance to get somethin' out of all my work and worry.'

Babe looked at him coldly.

'Babe,' Charlie said pleadingly, 'I never said anything to the Bearcat about you. I never told him how you picked all those other fighters clean. I never told him how you wrecked those guys.'

'Yeah,' said Babe. 'And I never told the Bearcat how you tried for three hours to make me up in Toni's one time.'

'For God's sake, Babe,' Charlie begged. 'Do you want me to get down on my knees to you?'

'No,' said Babe. 'You needn't bother to-night.'

'Listen, Babe, if you'll just lay off the Bearcat till after this fight, you can do what you want with him. If he wins, he'll have plenty of jack. But if he loses, he won't be no good no more. He won't get a crack at the champeenship – he won't be no good to me or you.'

'Well,' said Babe. 'Why the hell didn't you talk like this when you first came in instead of threatenin' me? I ain't got a heart of stone. I can listen to reason. But hell, nobody in this world can bully me into somethin'.'

Charlie brightened.

'Then you will keep away from the Bearcat till after this fight?'

Babe looked at Charlie for a moment. She tried to read Charlie's intentions. What was behind his sudden change of tactics, she wondered. She could not figure him out.

'I'll think it over,' she said slowly.

'You're a sport!' cried Charlie.

The telephone rang. Babe lifted the receiver.

'Hello,' she said. Then she shot a glance at Charlie. 'Come back in about ten minutes. I'll be ready then. All right.' She hung up.

'Babe,' said Charlie, 'if I can ever do anything for you, let me know.'

'Now get to hell out of here, you rat! I'll see you later.'

Charlie got.

Outside, Charlie wiped the perspiration from his face. 'God, what a job,' he thought. 'If she don't come through after me doin' the sob stuff and turnin' on the water-works, I'm licked.' Then he grinned. 'She's the kind of a jane any guy might fall for. If it wasn't for this racket, I wouldn't mind havin' her myself.'

As he stepped out of the lift and entered the lobby he saw the Bearcat sitting in one of the chairs. He was startled at seeing his manager. Charlie walked over to him.

'Thought you was stretchin' out up in your room.'

'I'm meetin' some pals,' said the Bearcat. 'Takin' a little air before I turn in. What you doin here?'

'Same thing. Only I'm just quittin' 'em. I got somethin' to say to you before you hit the hay.'

'All right,' the Bearcat responded.

That night in Charlie's room, the Bearcat sat on the edge of the bed, while Charlie talked.

'Week from to-night, you're goin' to be standin' in the road' – Charlie pointed to the autographed champions on the walls – 'that them fellows there walked to a barrel of gold – or you'll be a hard-luck story for a dime magazine. From now on, Bearcat, you turn in at ten every night and cut out this Gordon woman.'

'What do you mean?'

'Just what I said.'

'What do you know about — '

Charlie interrupted.

'It's too early in the game for a good pug to mix a woman with his fightin'.'

'What are you talkin' about?'

'I'm talkin' about Babe Gordon. I don't want you to feel bad, kid, but all the sap and guts and iron brain you got can't be wasted in any love clinches.'

'Why, there ain't nothin' wrong between us, Charlie.'

'Well, if there ain't yet, there will be. I know Babe. Yes, sir, I know what I'm talkin' about. Stick with her and you'll wish you were dead. Anyway, kid, if I see you with her until you've won his fight, I'm going to cancel the bout. And that goes, if she even so much as comes into the gym while you're trainin'. One o'clock, kid. This ain't no time for you to be up.'

7

◆◇◆

THE PATH OF GLORY

HARLEM JOE HASTINGS stooped through the ropes and stepped on the white canvas square. A mighty shout went up from the packed arena – a black and white political, sporting, and social assemblage. Jewelled white women bravoed and waved handkerchiefs beside smartly groomed black companions. Babe sat in a ringside seat, in a thousand dollars' worth of clothes, a black broadcloth wrap with a bushed fox collar, a smart black hat pressed down on marcelled gold.

Her face was calm ivory and her lips tinted. It was a vastly different Babe from the shop-worn girl who on the occasion of Bearcat's first fight in Harlem had been the centre of jeering attention and cheap wise-cracks. This was a transformed Babe with a poise and assurance discovering a place in the social register. The old-timers kept quiet. Her appearance awed them. She was some Tammany politician's woman, they surmised, far too high socially to be kidded in public.

Bearcat received an ovation as he slipped through the ropes, electrical energy in white insulation. Babe looked at him with the satisfaction of a trapper exhibiting a captured animal. Triumph over this man gave a conquering sparkle to her eye. She watched the Bearcat with the consuming pride of possession.

The crowd was on hair-trigger excitement. It was an even money bet as to the winner. Harlem had dug up its last dollar to back its favourite. Seconds were rubbing up circulation over the Bearcat's body. Determination, calm courage, and smiling bravery radiated from him. Joe Hastings, none the less calm and confident, appeared if anything more formidable as he slipped off his purple bathrobe.

He was a glamorous negro with a yellow-black body, fully developed calves and thighs, long gangling arms and an almost femininely slender torso. His road to successive victories was by way of his long reach, piston-like blows, and punch-proof head. He moved like a panther and had endeared himself to coloured worship by a famous water-melon grin.

The two contrasting bodies came to the ring centre, clasped gloves and received final instructions. The human throng pulled up taut and tense, to feast upon this supreme battle of black and white. The gong rang!

The two bodies rushed at each other and became a whirlpool of stabbing, slashing arms, swirling like angry foam in a boiling rapids, now white, now muddy black – a gush of red blood in the foam – the white form of Bearcat sank to the canvas. The jungle wrenched up from the arena in a screaming howl.

'You got him, black boy!'

'Kill him!'

'Keep him down!'

'He's ready for the cooler!'

The arm of the referee began tolling off the count.

Charlie Yates turned one sick look at Babe, smiling coldly at the misfortune before her, her eyes as indifferent as if she were viewing a strange corpse. Then at the count of nine a lightning bolt of white shot up from the canvas and sped into the black body. It sagged, cracking like a stick of charcoal, to the platform. A mad delirium of cheering rocked the arena, and waves of tensioned talk rose like a tide over the tiers, as the bell clanged, ending the round and saving Harlem Joe from being counted out.

Friends were pounding the bewildered Charlie on the back and shoulders. Babe sat quiet and studied the Bearcat with searching attention.

The bell sounded for round two.

Black human shrubbery bent forward in the square pit; a thousand eyes gleaming like jet spangles against the cyclorama of black looked on with hushed attention. On the roped raft under the sharp light, pale and dark flesh seesawed, tugged, strained, wrenched, pounded, staggered dizzily and blindly sputtered back and forth like sparks in a candle flame, with the white wick of the referee's arm always breaking them up.

Round after round of this remorseless, unrelenting impact. Charlie was crouched back in his chair, hands clenched over his knees in a sweaty grip. Babe's face was a grave mask. The coloured boy had had the best of it since that cannon-cracker first round.

A crash of flesh! The jungle was on its haunches again in a fury of noise, like smashing locomotives. The white body was pitched into the ropes and Joe Hastings rushed at it to pound it into unconsciousness. Charlie went pale with agony. Babe did not stir; her face was like cold steel.

Hastings swung and missed as the Bearcat dropped to his knees. The Bearcat staggered out to the open space, Hastings bearing down on him mercilessly. Lunging, swaying, zigzagging, Bearcat drifted along the ropes, Hastings doggedly following with desperate swings and uppercuts.

The din was ear-splitting. Bearcat suddenly stood firm in the centre of the ring, set for one supreme effort. A straight left crashed into the astonished black body. Hastings sank slowly to the canvas but not before a smashing right had crossed to the jaw. The four slopes quivered with an earthquake that ripped wide cracks in that human mountain of black lava. The referee's arm pumped up and down with the count. It came to a stop.

Harlem Joe Hastings still slumbered.

The Bearcat's gloved hand was raised in victory.

Another K.O. was added to his record.

The Bearcat sat in his dressing-room, which was jammed with eager questioning reporters, while his trainer and seconds were applying gauze bandages to his battered body. His face was scraped to red round-steak, one eye shut tight, lips swollen out of shape; and chest skinned in entirety in the desperate punishment he took during the last round. He merely nodded his head, yes or no, to the barrage of questions hurled at him by the sports writers.

'Will you challenge at once for the middleweight crown?'

A nod, 'Yes.'

'If you win the middleweight championship will you draw the colour line?'

A shake of the head, 'No.'

'Are you hurt much?' from a cub reporter.

The Bearcat tried his best to laugh.

'Will you marry?'

The door opened and Babe entered. The reporters crowded around her. Bearcat's one good eye smiled as big as it could. He reached out his right arm to her – the lamp-post that had piled up Harlem Joe on the kerbing. Babe smiled and patted his cheek. The reporters climbed about her.

'Are you his sweetheart?'

'If you are married, are there any children, or do you expect an offspring soon?'

'What was, or is, your maiden name?'

Here the manager intervened.

'You can leave all that bunk out!'

The surprised reporters turned to look. Charlie, grim-faced

and stern-eyed, was crunching his cigar under his heel and staring at Babe.

'That boloney don't fit in with the true story,' he said – 'the true story dope I'm commencin' in the *World*. You'll be gettin' your sheets in Dutch if you spill that line of apple mush.'

'Oh say, Charlie, you know we've got to get a story to-night. What's doing?'

'Well, you can take this statement from me and put it over my signature. The Bearcat ain't losin' his head and jeopardizin' his future by thinkin' of marriage with the usual bloodsucker parasites crashin' his dressin'-room.'

'That's hot – hot copy, boys.'

'Bearcat's manager K.O.'s romance for the big Bearcat.'

'Bearcat to stay wild.'

'Bearcat growls at chains of matrimony.'

The newspapermen went scuffing out.

The Bearcat was rinsing blood out of his mouth with listerine. Seconds and trainer were jamming fighting-gear into a suitcase. Charlie motioned them to leave. The trainer stopped in the door.

'See you to-morrow, Bearcat.'

The Bearcat turned thoughtfully to his trainer.

'Not for a couple of days.'

'See us both to-morrow in my room, Buck,' Charlie cut in.

'All right, I get ya,' Buck replied. The trainer saluted and left.

The Bearcat, humiliated and mortified at his manager's throwing strife into his victory, spoke up indignantly to Charlie.

'Hell of a way to congratulate a guy, bustin' in crazy like that. Lousiest I was ever treated in my life. Rawest thing ever pulled on me — '

'Wait a minute,' Charlie was sneering at Babe. 'Not half so lousy or raw as that dame's pullin' on me.'

'I don't want to fight no more to-night. Charlie,' the Bearcat murmured.

'You heard what I said to the newspaper guys, didn't you?' Charlie said to Babe.

'I don't mind an insult,' she said, 'when it ain't meant mean.'

'Well, I meant it the way said it. When I tell you it's walkin' papers for you, I mean it. Now scram!'

The Bearcat stiffened.

'That ain't no way to talk to somebody 'at helped me win this fight.'

Charlie's mouth looked nasty.

'And helped to wipe off a couple of thousand bucks out of your earnings for an evenin's flash of duds. And when she's gone through all you got she won't even pawn a piece of thread out of them rags to git you coffee-and.'

Babe smiled with a pretended wanness, looking into Bearcat's eyes.

'If I'm throwin' myself at you, Bearcat, I'll be removin' myself. I only wanted my friendship to be helpful to you.'

'It is, Babe.'

Charlie cut in with a snarl.

'That's up to my judgment. Bearcat Delaney's under contract to me and I'm the judge of what's the wise thing in his case. I told you what I expected from you, soon as this fight was over. If the Bearcat wants to bust his contract, that's different. You better be breezin' along. I got business with the kid.'

'I wouldn't have nobody break up a contract over me,' Babe said with apparent sincerity.

'No,' sneered Charlie. 'Not when it means dough to you.'

Babe paused near the door.

'If you only knew somethin' besides being hard-boiled, Charlie, you'd be a success. Congratulations, Bearcat. The trick stuff you pulled in the first and last rounds was pretty.

That's the kind of stuff your manager ought to give you all the time. Don't be bad friends over me.' Babe drifted out through the doorway.

The Bearcat moved as if to follow her, but then stopped and turned to Charlie. His voice had a hurt note in it.

'What the hell's got into you, Charlie?'

'Let's go to the hotel,' was the vague answer.

The lobby of the Nelson was filled with Charlie's friends – fighters, baseball players, theatrical managers – all dropping in to congratulate him on his new find. A well-known theatrical producer who had been a fight promoter himself told Charlie he hadn't seen anything as classy as the Bearcat since Sullivan.

The producer took them over to Reuben's for a bite, and there the future of the Bearcat was debated and prophesied to an indisputable certainty. Even the 'ifs' were not brought up as obstacles. Bearcat's future was measured with the yard stick of fame.

8

THE BEARCAT LOOKS IN
HIS MIRROR

THE Bearcat was moody and little interested in the plans these wise guys were drawing up for his future. He got no kick out of their extravagant flattery, so he was silent and sullen, wondering why in hell he couldn't be left alone to run his own life, at least in so far as Babe was concerned.

All he really cared about at the moment was the party planned to celebrate his victory, up in Joe Malone's hotel room, where the Babe was waiting.

There was no happiness for him in anything that could happen outside her realm. She had captured more than his body, for she dominated his thoughts and fired his imagination.

Charlie knew this and feared for the result. He knew that self-interest was the key to success. That where a world's championship was the objective, the aspirant had to concentrate selfishly on himself, that every atom of energy had to be carefully preserved to drive the will to the desired end. You had to conserve the whole of your vitality, guard it jealously, give none of yourself away.

The Bearcat pushed his chair back from the table; he had no appetite for food and even less for their talk. He explained that he wanted to go back to his hotel. Charlie could not leave his friends, and felt that Bearcat had had enough of his presence for that night. He hated to bear down on his fighter as he had done in that scene in the dressing-room at the fight club, but he congratulated himself that he had flattened out the Babe in the nick of time.

The Bearcat went to his hotel. As soon as he was inside his room he rushed to the telephone and called the hotel where Malone was staying.

'Give me Joe Malone's room.'

He waited.

'Hello, Joe? Bearcat. Babe there? No, I don't want to talk. Just say I'll be over. That's right. S'long.'

The Bearcat paced up and down the carpet twice and then pulled open the bureau drawers. He took out the shirt that Babe liked best, the soft collar that she was partial to, and the tie that pleased her.

He got into his snappiest suit.

Charlie had irritated him, depressed him – always holding him down, disciplining him, caging him. He didn't know just why but he actually dreaded Charlie, couldn't be at ease with him any more – felt himself evading any talk with him. He disliked the contemptuous twist of Charlie's mouth. All the things he had formerly admired and respected in Charlie he now questioned.

On the night of his big success when everything, every effort, should have been put forth to let him go loose a bit, give him a change from the bridle and check-rein, Charlie hands him a dirty humiliation before the girl he was crazy about, makin' him a laughin' stock in front of the reporters, mussin' his dignity so he couldn't talk. Now he was actually hating his manager.

Babe was oKay in every way. She was for him because she liked him. His mind went back to that first night he had met her, and afterwards in the cab. He thought of her long warm kisses. He trembled. She was all right. And whatever Charlie said, contract or no contract, the fact was that she had coached him to his victory by instilling in him a profound confidence in himself. He had knocked out the toughest proposition Harlem could put up. He had brought down a savage. Now he was of some importance. He had the stuff of conquerors in him, and conquerors weren't ruled like slaves, the way Charlie was trying to rule him. The Bearcat paled and gulped as he recalled the insult Charlie had hurled at Babe, and he had stood there dumb, not saying a word in defence of her honour.

Suddenly he walked to his mirror and surveyed himself. His face was puffed and marred with adhesive tape. 'Here I am alone in this room,' he thought, 'and success, cheers, victory – what have they brought me? What have I? Who have I? No one.'

He started pitying himself. He felt abused.

'What did Charlie care except for himself? Just the lousy dollar was all he wanted, and to go around braggin': "I made him. I put him over. I own him body and soul."'

'Would Charlie give up a woman that he loved? Would he give up a woman for me? Like hell! Bet if I went to his room now, I'd find a dame there. Here he goes denyin' me happiness when just seein' the woman I love is all I want. That's all I need.'

He looked again at his cut face reflected in the mirror. If she were here she'd kiss those bruises well. If I don't see her somebody else will. Hell, I can't stand it. I'm going to her. To hell with everybody else!

The Bearcat snatched up his hat from the bed and slammed the door as he dashed for the lift.

9

CELEBRATION

A MONTH ago, it was Charlie whom the Bearcat was grateful to, worshipped, and wanted to please . . . Charlie was God to him. He lived only to sweat and train and grind for Charlie; to be rewarded with an approving smile or, better still, a hand-shake and slap on the back. Now he wanted Babe's caresses – her kisses, the sweet joy of her nearness, for he loved her more dearly than pugilistic fame, more passionately than words could express.

The Bearcat entered Joe Malone's hotel and from the desk phoned up to Joe and announced his arrival. In another minute he was in the lift, had stepped out at the tenth floor, and rather breathlessly entered Joe's room.

Joe embraced him and kissed him on both raw cheeks in burlesque of French cordiality and then did a dance on the bedcovers.

'Bearcat!' he exclaimed with enthusiasm. 'That dump club ain't seen anythin' as classy as 'at mix to-night.'

Babe sat cameo'd against a blue velvet overstuffed chair, with an amber floor lamp shedding a soft glow on her smiling features.

The Bearcat went over to her.

'I want to apologize for Charlie's actin' crazy like that to-night, Babe,' he said, with a pleading look.

'That's all right, honey,' Babe said, placing her hand on his arm. 'Charlie gets excited and don't know what he's sayin'.'

Joe was tossing chunks of ice into three glasses.

'Charlie's a gaoler, I tell ya,' Joe commented. 'Yer under lock an' key alla time yer scrappin' for him. He don't let you have no life. Don't give you a chance to enjoy a dollar you make.' The white rock was sparkling on the ice in the glasses. 'What's t'use of makin' a million if you're tied down so's you can't enjoy it?'

Malone was for the spoils of victory. He expatiated further.

'A soldier gets a better break than a fighter wit' Charlie. Even a sailor gits shore leave and can raise hell. No sense to fightin' if there ain't a little sport wit' it. Ain't 'at right, Babe?'

'Sure,' said Babe. 'Charlie's gettin' away with murder. Tryin' to make out like he was a saint.'

Joe snorted.

'Ain't I seen him come up here paralysed drunk, many a time? You ask me, Babe, he's jealous over ya. Used to like ya a lot when he first knew you.'

Babe crossed to the radio.

'Let's not talk about Charlie, no more,' the Bearcat said. 'I'm here, ain't I? Don't that show you better than anythin' that I'm boss of my own life from now on, outside of trainin' hours?'

Babe tuned in a dance orchestra on the radio. Joe thrust a glass into her hand, and another into the Bearcat's. Then he raised his own.

'Here's to the nex' champ!'

The Bearcat laughed modestly. They drank.

Babe took the Bearcat's left hand and placed his right arm around her waist. They danced.

Joe looked at them, then taking a bottle and a glass he went into the bathroom and closed the door. Malone was a good pal. He was a fighter himself and realized what it meant to Bearcat to be alone with his girl.

As Babe and the Bearcat stood swaying rhythmically to the strain of a Spanish love song which came floating out of the radio, the Bearcat pressed her to him, kissed her soft golden hair, her lips, her throat. They forgot about Joe. He didn't exist for them. They might have been upon some island alone. The sensuous music ended but the Bearcat was swept on. He kissed Babe passionately and held her tighter to him.

The Bearcat had never known a sensation like this before. He couldn't think of anything, except Babe. He gazed deep into her eyes. He loved her, but he did not know how to tell her. His lips were mute under the compelling force of his inner passion. Did she feel the same as he, he wondered. He wanted to go on holding her and kissing her for ever.

Joe returned to the room, a little drunker than when he had left.

'Don't mind me, I know just how you feel,' he said.

'I don't think you do,' replied Bearcat. 'It's wonderful.' He thought no woman except the one he held in his arms could make a man feel that way. And he was sure that neither Joe nor any other man had ever held her just that way.

The three had a little supper together in the room. Joe had ordered it sent up. The Bearcat could not have made any elaborate plans to celebrate with Babe for it would have certainly got back to Charlie.

They sat there eating and drinking and talking, growing a little drunker as the night wore on. By and by, Babe began to be a little weary. She would have liked to go with the Bearcat at once. Everything would have been great had they been alone, even though Joe was a very congenial host. The Bearcat sat in the big chair with his arms around Babe, while Joe dragged out a book of Press clippings of himself, as he always did after a few drinks, and showed it to them. They were bored to death but pretended to be interested.

Then Babe suggested going home.

'Joe looks tired,' she said. 'We'd better be going.'

Joe denied it. 'No, I ain't. Stay a while. It's early yet.'

'No,' said Babe, 'you did enough for us to-night, Joe. We certainly appreciate it.'

'Yeah, Joe,' the Bearcat put in, 'you cert'n'y are a real pal.'

Babe put on her hat after arranging her hair, which badly needed a comb since the Bearcat had mauled it all evening. He had almost kissed the waves out of it.

'Aw right, Joe,' said the Bearcat, extending his hand, 'I'll see you to-morrow afternoon. Drop around to the hotel.'

'Sure,' Joe said, shaking hands. 'I'll see you all of a sudden. Good night, Babe, take care of him.'

'Take care of me?' Bearcat laughed. 'I'll take care of her.'

'That ain't what I mean,' said Joe enigmatically.

Down in the street, the Bearcat stepped up to a cab that stood by the kerb and threw open the door. Babe got in.

'Hotel Europe on 49th Street,' the Bearcat said to the driver, and followed her into the cab.

The taxi eased away from the hotel. Babe slipped her arm about the Bearcat's neck, pressed her cheek against his and relaxed her body into his lap.

The Bearcat felt the soft round mould of Babe's limbs. Her cheek against his felt cool and soothing. The touch of her soft body against his own raw, irritated flesh which had been scraped on the ring ropes was soothing – like the comforting rub-down of his trainer after a work-out. All these sensations were blended into one sweetness like that moment of blessed relief in the corner between rounds, when the senses were released in fleeting slumber before the gong signalled for renewed battle.

'You do care for me, don't you?' the Bearcat asked Babe.

'Oh, I'm crazy about you. You ought to know that by now.' Babe clung to him. 'I wouldn't let you kiss me like that if I didn't care a lot.'

'Do you like the way I kiss you?' The Bearcat's breath came quickly.

'I'm mad about it,' Babe whispered. 'Just don't stop, that's all.'

There was something sweet in woman's flesh that made a man's flesh thirsty and hungry and feverish and drunk all at the same time. The Bearcat had believed the supreme thrill to be the fierce joy of man's flesh grinding against man's flesh in ring combat. But he felt something different and new in that cab.

'I never did much of this,' he said. 'Kind of takes my breath away. I didn't know I could do it like this until to-night.'

Babe pressed her lips to his ear.

'You've kissed other girls before.'

'Never like this – and very few of them too.'

'Hell, what *would* Charlie say to all this?' The cab was passing the Nelson Hotel, right where Charlie was proudly waiting for his mighty warrior. The Bearcat went sick at heart passing the hotel. He sought to resist, hoped for the bell to save him, but the cab rolled on street after street with the Bearcat lost in sensuous bliss.

The Bearcat said good-night to Babe at the lift in her hotel. Then with his thoughts in a jumble he walked toward the corner. His hand happened into his pocket, and he pulled out an unfamiliar bulk. It was Babe's gloves – three-quarter-length white kid.

'Well, what do you know about that?' he asked himself.

He looked around, undecided what to do. There was a drug store on the corner which remained open all night. He went there, and into a telephone booth.

He called Babe's hotel and got her on the wire.

'I found your gloves in my pocket, dear,' he said.

'Where are you now, honey?' Babe asked.

'Right down at the corner at a drug store.'

'Oh,' said Babe. 'Then you better bring them to me. I might want to wear them to-morrow.'

He walked rapidly back to the hotel and entered the lift.

He was a bit nervous going up to her room. He felt that he was being watched. The Bearcat noticed that the coloured lift boy had some morning newspapers. A tabloid bore a huge picture of himself.

'Gimme that paper,' he told the boy. He dug out a dollar bill and gave it for the paper. 'Keep the change.'

The boy's face lit up with a friendly grin as he pocketed he money. Tips had been few that night.

'Yo' is Misto Delaney, ain't yo'?' he said. 'I done been readin' 'bout yo' in duh papers.'

'Yeah?' the Bearcat said, smiling. 'What does it say?'

'It says yo' is one gran' fighter, sho' enuff.'

'Well, that's good, ain't it?' The Bearcat was at a loss for words.

'Sho' is. What flo' yo' want, suh?'

'Five.'

The coloured boy bowed him off.

He knocked cautiously at Babe's door. It opened at once. Babe was in an underslip and about to put on a négligé. He took her in his arms and commenced kissing her.

'I'm glad you came back, dear,' she said.

'You are? Ain't it too late to have company in your room?'

'Oh, that's all right,' Babe said, with a wave of her hand. 'They know me in this hotel. I'm not used to havin' gentlemen come up. Besides, the house dick is a good friend of mine. He wouldn't bother me. He's a right guy.'

'It's all right then?'

'Sure, honey. The only time they bother you is when they think you ain't respectable and throw wild parties.'

• • • • •

When morning whitened the drawn shades, the Bearcat awoke.

He bent over and kissed Babe gently. Her eyes opened. Then she smiled.

'Honey,' he said, 'do you care for me now as you did before?'

Babe placed her arms around his neck.

'I'm mad about you.'

'When you say that, you mean you love me?'

She wondered what he was up to.

'I guess I do, honey.'

The Bearcat held her close.

'Well, I want to know for sure, dear. 'Cause I love you so much I never want to be away from you again.'

'That's a good one for Charlie,' said Babe, with a little laugh.

'When I make up my mind to anythin', Charlie or nobody else can't change it.'

He kissed her again, held her tightly for an instant, and then sprang up and started to dress.

Babe lay there, wondering silently: 'Why the rush?'

Soon dressed, the Bearcat came over to the bed, bent down and kissed her.

'I'll be back in a half-hour, dear.'

And he was out of the door and gone before Babe could say a word or question him about his actions.

Joe Malone sprang out of bed at the sound of the bell. He came out of unpleasant dreams and was relieved that the bell he heard was the telephone ringing, and not one summoning him to another smashing round. He still felt groggy from last night's bout with the bottle.

It was Bearcat calling him, and there was enthusiasm and a wild happiness in his voice.

'How you feelin', Joe?'

'Great!' said Joe, forgetting his aching head.

'I want you to do me a favour, Joe.'

'Yeah?'

'I want you to meet me over in Babe's hotel as quick as you can.'

'Why, what's happened?' Joe cried in surprise. 'Anythin' wrong?'

'No,' came back Bearcat's voice over the wire. 'Everything's great. She loves me – and you know – well, I want you to be the best man.'

Joe was stunned.

'What? You don't mean to tell me — '

'Yeah – we're goin' over to Jersey and do it. Now hurry up. Make it snappy!'

Before Joe could utter another word the Bearcat had hung up, and was on his way to a jewellery store, where he bought the necessary ring. Then, slipping his two-and-a-half-carat diamond ring off his finger, he handed it to the jeweller.

'How long will it take you to put that in a lady's setting?'

'Not long,' the jeweller said. 'I'll do it right away.'

The jeweller showed him a tray of beautiful settings to select from. The Bearcat chose one he hoped Babe would like.

From there he went to the barber's, where in a short time he had everything in the place done to him. Hair cut, shave, massage, tonic. All the extras.

Then he purchased a clean collar and new tie and started for the hotel.

In the meantime, Joe Malone had snapped into his best clothes, drunk two or three eye-openers and a cup of black coffee, and dashed into the street, catching a cab on the fly, as it were. He arrived at Babe's room before the Bearcat had returned.

Babe had not yet started to get dressed. She was surprised at his visit, not knowing the import of it.

'Well, kid,' Joe said with a broad grin, 'accept me best wishes. You sure are a smart broad.'

Babe's eyes widened.

'What do you mean?'

'Why, I mean marryin' a guy like the Bearcat.'

'We ain't married.'

'I know that,' said Joe. 'But the Bearcat just called me up and says we're hoppin' over to Jersey for you two to get tied. I'm standin' up for ya.'

Babe stood still, looking at Joe. Now she knew what the Bearcat was driving at with his, 'Do you love me, or don't you love me?' stuff. She hadn't quite figured on marrying him. But – why not? She liked him a lot, and besides he was in the money and would be in plenty more when he knocked off the champion.

'Well, Joe,' she said – 'we was goin' to keep it a secret. But as long as the Bearcat told you, I might as well admit it. Yes, we're gettin' married.'

'Babe,' said Joe, 'you're walkin' right into a mess of dough. An' look at the publicity.'

'Yeah,' said Babe, 'if Charlie don't try to ruin everything.'

'Well, I guess it will hit Charlie kind of hard. But, what the hell, you'll be married. He ain't got no comeback. An' he's been plannin' too long for the championship fight to kick up a fuss now.'

Babe began dressing. Her nerves had always been the best, but now with the prospect of immediate marriage staring her in the face, she felt a bit shaky inside.

The Bearcat came bounding into the room, his face as red and glowing as a harvest moon.

'Look, dear,' he cried, after greeting Joe briefly. His hand brought a small jewellery box from his pocket. He opened it and drew the reset diamond from it. He took Babe's hand.

"Oh, Bearcat, honey!' Babe exclaimed with delight as he slipped the ring on the third finger of her left hand. She kissed him.

'Like it, Babe?' he asked, anxiously watching her face.

'It's beautiful. Oh, you're a darling.'

She kissed him again, and he held her for a long minute.

'Time!' called Joe, with a laugh.

They broke.

'Gee, I almost forgot. I got a swell car downstairs waitin' to take us to Jersey. You better hurry, dear.'

Babe disappeared into the bathroom. The Bearcat changed his collar and tie, whistling all the while.

Joe watched him, a cigarette dangling from his mouth.

'Bearcat,' he said, 'you're a lucky guy, to grab off a girl like Babe. I know guys 'at would lay down at her feet just for the chance of her walkin' on 'em.'

'Am I happy? Am I happy? Boy, you can tell the world I am!' The Bearcat did a little jig.

'You oughter be,' Joe said. He was going to say something about Charlie, but changed his mind.

Babe was soon ready and the three piled into the waiting motor-car. The Bearcat tilted his hat at a jaunty angle and gave the chauffeur directions.

They didn't talk much on that journey. In Jersey City, the Bearcat's home town, they found a justice of the peace who was willing to make a few dollars. And before noon they were married.

A happy, big-boy expression lighted the Bearcat's face as Babe received the wedding-ring on her finger. When the ceremony was over, the Bearcat gathered Babe in his arms.

'Under new management,' she said, and kissed him.

The Bearcat was feeling great. He laughed heartily and took out a roll of bills from which he peeled a yellow-back and passed it to the justice.

'There you are, judge,' he said. 'For the uppercut you just put over on us.'

'Thank you, and good luck,' said the justice, as he took the money and handed Babe the marriage certificate.

Babe smiled and thanked the justice as they left.

The judge said: 'Good-bye, folks. I wish you lots of happiness.'

Joe had to speak his piece.

'Good-bye, judge. I might come over to see you myself some time. You can't never tell.'

On the return the car sped with a wet, sticky sound through the Holland Tunnel. The policemen stationed at intervals in the tunnel grinned as they saw the two locked in each other's arms on the back seat.

'What's the programme now?' Joe inquired, after they had come out on the New York side.

'Back to the hotel,' the Bearcat said.

'I mighter known that,' Joe said with a snicker. 'I guess you won't need me around from now on.'

'Oh, stick around,' the Bearcat told him. 'We'll have a little weddin' dinner and a few drinks as soon as we get settled.'

'Drinks?' Joe pricked up his ears. 'Well in that case I'll come along.'

Babe first checked out of the Hotel Europe, then they engaged a suite at the Vandermore, a more exclusive uptown hotel.

Once in their new quarters the Bearcat became preoccupied. How was he going to break the news to Charlie? Always Charlie. Always having to worry, 'What will Charlie say? What will Charlie think? What will Charlie do?' He was sick of it.

'Babe,' he said, 'we got to break the news to Charlie.'

'Yeah,' Babe replied, 'we got to tell him.'

Joe butted in with the comment:

'Aw, don't worry about him. Get him on the phone and tell him to come over here. Then he can hang up on you, if he gits sore.'

The Bearcat went to the phone and called the Nelson. Charlie was in the lobby wondering why the Bearcat had not returned to the hotel the night before. He felt something was up.

'Hello – Charlie?' said the Bearcat.

'Hello,' said Charlie, 'where the hell are you?'

'I'm up at the Vandermore. I want you to come over. I got somethin' important to talk to you about.'

'All right,' Charlie agreed. He wanted to get to the bottom of this right away.

'Suite one thousand and nine,' the Bearcat informed him.

On his way to the Vandermore, Charlie pondered the situation. He had come to no conclusion when he rapped at apartment one thousand and nine.

Joe opened the door.

'You here, Malone?' Charlie snapped.

'Oh, I'm always around somewheres, Charlie,' Joe answered maliciously.

"Yeah, where there's trouble,' Charlie said icily. The Bearcat stood nervously in the centre of the room, Babe sat in a chair by the window, the afternoon sun lighting her face and almost too golden hair.

'Hello, Charlie,' greeted the Bearcat. He extended his hand shyly.

Charlie gripped it hard. A thin, wintry smile flickered on his features.

'Hello, Bearcat,' he said; and then he saw Babe. He thought to himself: 'What's the game now?'

'I – I want you to wish us luck, Charlie,' the Bearcat was saying.

'Hey?' inquired Charlie, uncomprehending.

'Sure, wish 'em luck, Charlie,' Joe put in. 'The kids are crazy about each other. Wish 'em luck. You always was a sport.'

Babe extended her left hand to him. The sun caught the diamond and sent myriad points of light into Charlie's eyes.

He took her hand. He saw the two rings. He could hardly believe his eyes.

Charlie went white. As he squeezed her hand, he wished to God it was her neck he was squeezing. His mind whirled.

'The dirty little tart! After all my pleadin' last week. I hate her guts!' The blood surged to his head. He sat down heavily in a chair without a word.

They all saw something was wrong with Charlie, but they tried to pass it off.

'I'm glad you take it this way, Charlie,' said the Bearcat. 'You'll see, I'll be better than ever. I'll make everything up to you, Charlie, for your worry. I'll train like the devil every day. Babe will help me. I'll show you, Charlie.'

Charlie's mind began to clear. If he had only known of this before, he'd have moved heaven and earth to stop it. But he hadn't figured that she'd go so far as to marry the Bearcat.

'Charlie,' the Bearcat said pleadingly, 'I ain't pulled nothin' crooked on you. This ain't got nothin' to do with fightin'. It's somethin' personal. Somethin' between me and myself. Somethin' that's deep in here.' He pressed his hand against his heart.

Charlie's eyes were still focused on the blue sky beyond the window.

The Bearcat's arms dropped loosely to his sides. His shoulders drooped.

'I guess you don't see it my way,' he said. 'I guess I'm kicked out." His voice became hoarse. 'All right, Charlie, if that's how you feel. I'll be packin'.'

Charlie's eyes swept around to him. His voice was almost a whisper.

'You ain't pulled nothin' crooked, kid. But you might have told me. It hurts to be let down like this. But it's all right, kid. It's done. I ain't one to squawk over what's past. You're too decent a sap to think of your own good. And I ain't blamin' you for not knowin' what you ain't found out. I hope it's all like you think, kid. I hope it is. It sounds swell, the way Mrs. Delaney might be able to help you. It could be that way, and I'd like to see it that way. I'm with you. I like you. Miracles happen, sometimes. But we'll see who's with you at the finish and what the finish is. I'm reservin' my congratulations till then. See you to-morrow at the gym, ten sharp.'

Charlie rose and without another word walked out of the door and closed it softly behind him.

10

HONEYMOON

BABE and the Bearcat went right in for being big shots. Cokey Jenny and the gang in Toni's back room were cut dead. Big stuff, or nothing at all, as Babe put it. It was one thing after another, that whirl of high life. Races and ball games in the afternoon, theatres and suppers at night for Babe and the Bearcat's pals of the fighting fraternity, with nothing but the highest price booze.

But there was sense to all this splurging, Bearcat was convinced. Babe was the inspiration of a round of parties that was heading him for solid popularity and fame. There was insight and method in her entertainments. He could see that, plain as water. Babe was a brilliant social success, an irresistible hostess. Everybody liked her. Everybody came to pay homage to her. That's what counted.

He imagined it was the influence of her charm and priceless personality that was lifting him into the limelight, building him into a commanding figure, weaving prominence about him, making him colourful.

Of course the news of their marriage immediately got into the papers. It was hot stuff and the tabloids ate it up. Charlie was wild every time he picked up a paper and saw Babe's name connected with the Bearcat. She was taking space that Charlie wanted for his promotion schemes.

The Bearcat put some money down as a first payment on a snappy roadster with a rumble seat. His intention was to pay up the remainder with part of the winnings in his coming fight, for his bank roll was dwindling under an avalanche of bills. He taught Babe to drive the car and they made quite a flash with it.

Everywhere they went Babe shared the spotlight with Bearcat. Race track powers, ball players, actors, theatre managers were shaking hands with him, many of them dropping in at the apartment for a sociable drink of something 'real', or sending around flowers and candy to Babe.

They kept open house while Charlie was negotiating the bout which was to win Bearcat the middleweight championship.

Charlie spent hours cautioning the Bearcat against fast living, for well he knew that booze melted the iron concentration in the brain so vital to success, and he feared the effect on the Bearcat's stamina of this marriage which he would have done anything to prevent. The Bearcat was already taking on waist and losing the vital glow of health.

The day set for the big fight drew near, and suddenly the Bearcat realized that he could not continue the fast pace. He had been spending only two and three days a week training since he was married. The rest of the time he got to bed too late to get down to the gym at an early hour, and he always felt sluggish and languid after a night of dissipation. Charlie was furious, and insisted that he spend at least two weeks in the country at his training camp.

So Bearcat said to Babe one morning:

'I think, honey, that I better start and do some hard trainin'. It's gettin' near the big fight an' I want to win it – for you. Pack up my togs. I'm going to work for Charlie and pound the roads for two weeks.'

The days passed rapidly in a final spurt of intensive training. But his mind was none too clear, as he was uneasy about Babe, wondering what would happen if they could no longer continue their luxurious living. He had doubts. And they are very bad for a fighter.

The night of the fight arrived. Madison Square Garden was packed to the rafters. The ovation he received as he stepped into the ring was like crashes of thunder. The sports writers looked at him and whispered among themselves. They wondered what ailed him. He didn't look so good. In fact, all through his training they had thought something was wrong. His opponent was in prime condition. After the second round the question went around the arena: 'What is the matter with the Bearcat to-night?'

The fans received their answer when at the end of the fifteen rounds the decision was made against him.

Only the final bell had saved him from collapsing in that last round. Only sheer nerves had kept him on his feet.

The Bearcat had lost his chance for the championship!

11

TRUE COLOURS

CHARLIE beat the wall of the Bearcat's dressing-room in futile rage. He almost foamed at the mouth. All his hopes had vanished like smoke to-night. And all because of a woman.

He watched the Bearcat in dreadful silence while the latter was being rubbed down on the table, and when the work was finished he ordered the trainer and seconds to go.

Buck, the trainer, and the seconds had been as kind to Bearcat as they could. They tried to comfort him with words of encouragement which they were unable to make ring true. When they were gone, Charlie, who was pacing furiously up and down the room, stopped in front of the Bearcat, who was making a half-hearted attempt to dress.

The Bearcat had never seen such an ugly look on Charlie's face. Murder looked out of his eyes.

'Didn't I tell you so?' Charlie almost shrieked. 'Didn't I tell you if you went off your nut and tied up to that Gordon skirt your fightin' days were numbered? You remember what I told you over the phone, the night you laid out Harlem Joe. I knew you were at the hotel boozin' up with her. Now don't tell me you weren't. I guess it's a manager's business to keep his eye on the private life of a pug. I said, "Ditch that flashy Gordon tramp."'

Bearcat was out of his chair and his arm drove viciously at Charlie. Charlie side-stepped and the Bearcat sat down again and rubbed his forehead bewilderedly. The manager waited until the Bearcat's fury had subsided.

'I told you she's worked every black and white fighter in Harlem that looked like money.'

'Shut up your mug, Charlie.'

Charlie continued relentlessly.

'And none of 'em got even as far as a preliminary in the Garden after she got her hooks into them.'

'You tried to make her yourself, Charlie,' the Bearcat said defensively, quivering with a tortured fury. 'I got plenty evidence you were playin' up to her.'

Charlie stiffened.

'Ah, what the hell are you talkin' about? I never made a wrong crack to her. I know that wench's history. Why, goddam it, she's been pickin' up her meat in the fight ring since she was kicked out of school. Just lookin' for someone who'll think he's havin' a good time while she's gettin' their coin, like any hustler . . . Why that lousy broad —'

The Bearcat reared up from his chair.

'Damn you, Charlie! She's my wife, no matter what an' you can't talk about her like that. We're through, Charlie – through for good. See!'

Charlie's face was a mask of scorn.

'I'll say you're through, if you don't can this —'

The Bearcat cut him short.

'You've said enough. I ain't askin' you to spill no more. Get me?'

'No. I don't get you at all. When the hell are you snappin' out of your grog, and breakin' the clinch with this here bum? Where's your common-sense? If you think you're so goddam smart, just ask yourself what she's done with the championship that was as good as yours, the night you set the sport world on fire up in Harlem, with the big final? You were class then. And what've you done? Chucked it all overboard for a slut – a woman that's taken all the steam out of your system and sent you down for the count. You wanted me to wish you luck when you got married, wanted me to congratulate you. For what? For this? She'll pull you down to a ham fighter beggin' for ten dollar bouts. Through? You said it, kid.'

'You're just sore 'cause I married Babe,' the Bearcat growled.

'Bein' married is all right – I ain't complainin' about that. I wouldn't mind if you married the right kind of a woman. There's plenty of fighters that's married and got families, too, but their wives are helpful to 'em. Take good care of them; see that they eat right and lead a regular life; they don't wear 'em out. They're not good-time mammas like this dame you're hitched up to.' As Charlie got up he said: 'But, aw nuts! what's the use of talkin' about it? What's done is done.'

He walked to the door. Then his attitude underwent a change. He laughed. A note of derision was in it. It sent a chill up the Bearcat's spine.

'So this is love! A goddam belly-ache, that's what it is!' The door slammed after him.

Outside, Charlie brushed against Malone who was headed for the Bearcat's dressing-room.

'Tough break,' Malone said to him.

'Yeah, ain't it?' Charlie replied with a sneer. This was the third fighter Babe Gordon had spoiled for him, and the Bearcat had really been championship stuff. When he thought of it, the desire to kill entered his heart. 'I've never wanted to hit a woman in my life before, but if I meet that dame now, I'll break her jaw. Damn her soul to hell! It's enough to bust a guy wide open!'

He avoided friends and reporters as he walked morosely to his hotel.

Malone found the Bearcat sitting with his head in his hands. The Bearcat had never cried since he had been a child, but he certainly felt like it now. Malone placed his hand on his shoulder.

'It's the breaks of the game, kid,' he said. 'Too bad. But the next time you'll make up for it. Say, Babe's all broke up over it. She's waitin' for you out in the car. She felt too bad to come in. I'll go out and sit with her a while. How long you gonna be?'

The Bearcat raised his head for the first time and looked at Joe.

'I'll be right out, Joe.'

Joe didn't wait for him.

The Bearcat sat in a daze. What had happened? Where was the admiring crowd? Where were the slaps on the back? Where the newspapermen, questioning him about his future plans? He was alone in his dressing-room. What was the matter with him? He just couldn't get started to-night. Maybe, after all, Charlie was right.

Babe kissed him when he joined her and Malone in the car. She was driving.

'How about goin' down to Jack's Chop House for a while?' she suggested. 'Just to have a few drinks to quiet your nerves and cheer you up. Sittin' around the hotel room will give you the blues.'

'All right,' the Bearcat acquiesced. 'Anywhere you say. Maybe you're right. A couple of drinks would help, the way I feel now.'

'Sure,' said Malone. 'No use gettin' yourself stewed up over what can't be helped.'

'But it could be helped, Joe,' said the Bearcat. 'I had no business to lose that fight. I don't know what the devil's the matter with me.'

Babe slowed up for a traffic light.

'Can't Charlie get you a return engagement?'

'Charlie and me is through!'

'Don't be foolish,' Babe said quickly. 'Tell him you was sick or something. Let him spread it in the papers that you wasn't feelin' right when you went into the ring. Took sick all of a sudden. Charlie could fix up another match!'

'Maybe you're right, Babe. I'll talk to Charlie about it. But gee, I hate to face him after what we just went through in the dressin'-room. He said some pretty awful things about you, Babe.'

'Well, you don't believe them, do you?'

'Of course not, honey. I told him where he got off.'

'Well, see him to-morrow anyway. He'll be sorry for what he said then.'

'Sure he will,' Joe Malone put in. 'Charlie's a good guy at heart.'

Bearcat looked Charlie up at the Nelson the next day. His manager's anger had melted away overnight, but his manner was decidedly chilly as he opened the door of his room to greet the near champion.

The Bearcat was embarrassed as to how to begin.

'Charlie,' he said nervously, 'I – I wasn't feelin' myself when I went in there last night.'

'You tellin' me somethin'?' Charlie inquired frigidly.

'Now listen, Charlie. I mean I wasn't sleepin' right the last few nights before the fight. An' I think I overtrained.'

Charlie took his cigar from his mouth.

'Overtrained? The trouble was you didn't train enough.'

'Well, anyway, whatever it was, I felt knotted up and stiff-like and couldn't get up steam. But, Charlie, when I'm right I can put him in the shade in no time. I had him goin' till the sixth round. You saw that. If I was feelin' myself I would've knocked him out sure. Can't you get me another match with him, Charlie? I know I can lick him next time. I'll be in the gym every day with you watchin', and I'll hit the hay regular. Can't you say I was sick – had a touch of ptomaine poisonin' and now that I been to the hospital I'm a hundred per cent again? Tell 'em I was battlin' under a handicap in the last fight, really too sick to put up my mits.'

'Time to 'a' thought of that was before the fight. I never handled an alibi fighter in my life and I won't now.' There was a steel ring in Charlie's voice. 'I told you how I felt about things. I don't see anythin' more for you and me. Time for us to wash up.'

The Bearcat stood silent for a moment. Charlie's rebuff had stung him deeply. He swallowed his pride and said:

'Don't say that, Charlie. Fix me up some fights until I show you and everybody I got plenty left to whip the champ and to spare.'

'All right.' An impatient frown deepened on Charlie's forehead. 'I'll fix you to fight Sailor Reagan, week from now at the Coliseum. He's tough and fast. Just the boy to get the ptomaine out of your system.'

Bearcat overlooked the cutting insinuation on account of the gratitude that swept over him.

'That's great, Charlie. Couple a months I'll be champ. See if I ain't. So long.' Bearcat hurried out feeling sure of himself again. Charlie lit a fresh cigar, combed his hair in the mirror, and thought: 'That bastard Babe! And this kid was no flash in the pan either. She ought to be knocked off.' Charlie went to eat by himself.

The Bearcat, in spite of conscientious training, could not get back to form. He got a draw with Sailor Reagan when he should have outclassed him in every round. He couldn't understand it himself. He simply hadn't the energy to crush his antagonist with the old reserve power. Then he lost several fights to second-raters and found it difficult to get even a preliminary match.

His whole career was taking on an aspect of catastrophe. His showings were not only disappointing, they were making him look ridiculous. At the hotel, his old friends made excuses for him, patted him on the back sympathetically, cheered him with insincerities like: 'Next time, Bearcat.' 'Why, you're as good as you ever were.' But Bearcat was no longer the centre of an admiring throng, and he felt injured and abused.

Babe knew that up in Harlem the Bearcat was regarded with contempt. He was laughed at as a 'farce', a 'lemon' and a 'bust'. Of course, his money was still buying her dresses, but his funds were getting low. His glamour was tarnishing and she was losing interest, becoming more indifferent toward him every day. The world loves a hero and success, and Babe couldn't be bothered with a fallen idol. Her life with Bearcat had grown stale.

As he kept slipping, he reached out to her for comfort like a drowning man to a straw. Her body was the refuge where he could drown remorse and bury disappointment. But Babe was fed up. She was afraid to break with the Bearcat too suddenly. She knew that in a twinkling he could be transformed into a brute and with all his primitive passion roused could crush her to subordination.

Well, Bearcat couldn't go on much longer. He was almost at the end of his rope.

Several days after he had lost his most recent fight, the Bearcat walked into the hotel room and sat down on the bed. Babe was ready to go out. They said nothing to each other for a few minutes. Babe was adjusting her hat.

The Bearcat watched her.

'Better wait,' he said. 'I got something to say to you.'

Babe turned from the mirror and looked at him. 'What's the matter? The next fight off?'

'It's a whole lot more important than that.'

'I didn't know there could be anythin' more important than a match right now.'

The Bearcat looked uncomfortable.

'Well, there is. I'm through fightin'.'

'Yeah?' A surprised look flared up in Babe's eyes.

'Charlie's through with me.'

She was stark silent. Her eyes searched the Bearcat's weary face intently, and her mind seemed to be racing ahead of his to trap his thought.

'Well, can't you get no fights without Charlie?'

'No.'

'How about out west? Maybe you could get some good fights out there. They never saw you there, and if you trained hard, with all the publicity you got you might be a drawin' card. You could knock over a few of them palookas and then make a come-back here in the east.'

'That's no good, Babe. All the real matches are made here. It'd be just a waste of time goin' west. But that ain't what I wanted to tell you about.'

'No?' Babe wondered what he had up his sleeve. She regarded him narrowly.

The Bearcat seemed to draw a deep breath.

'I wanted to tell you,' he said, 'that I got rid of the car.'

She took a step toward him in amazement.

'Got rid of the car?'

'Yeah, Babe. I had to do it.'

Anger blazed up in her.

'What do you mean, you had to do it?' Her tone became bitterly sarcastic. 'So you got rid of the car without askin' me? Well, you got one hell of a nerve. I thought that car belonged to me. Didn't you buy it for me? I suppose I don't mean a goddam thing around here. I'm only your wife. You just do as you please with the car you got for me, and I got to walk, eh?'

The Bearcat was numb with astonishment. He had never heard Babe use such language before, except, perhaps, when she couldn't get a telephone number right away, or when the waves came out of her hair, or when she had trouble getting a tight shoe on. But she always excused her language afterwards very prettily.

'But, Babe,' he gasped, 'you won't have to do walkin'.'

'You're damn right I won't,' Babe almost shouted.

'Listen, Babe,' he said, trying to pacify her. 'I traded the car in for a taxicab.'

'You what?' She was speechless with anger for a moment. Then: 'Oh, so I ain't gonna walk. I'm gonna ride in a taxi. What do you expect me to do, ride up front with you? God, what a dope!'

'Aw, listen, Babe,' the Bearcat cried. 'I only did it for you. I want to make some money, till I get pulled together again. Only for a while. I'll get out and hustle with the cab. It'll be better for us both. We'll be livin' regular and accordin' to schedule and we'll soon be on our feet again. Believe me, Babe, I'm only doin' it for you.'

Babe's anger cooled. She felt a sudden pity for him, but at the same time her busy mind was active with a new scheme.

She spoke in a kinder tone.

'Look, Bearcat,' she said, 'how we're tied down. And I couldn't take the dough I need from you after you sweatin' for it chasin' fares. It wouldn't be right. I wouldn't be a burden to you like that.' She didn't exactly mean what she told him, for her thoughts were speculating on something else.

The Bearcat was delighted that she began to see things in a different light.

'Regular hours and keepin' to ourselves for a while is goin' to do us good like nothin' else. I'll make my shifts so I can take you to as many shows as you want to see.'

Babe had thought out something and the strain in her eyes relaxed.

'I wouldn't think of takin' advantage of you like that,' she told him. 'Usin' up your hard-earned dough for my amusement – unless I helped you.'

'How do you mean?' he asked.

'I mean, if I found somethin' to do, too. Maybe I could go back to Goldstein or some place else and model.'

The Bearcat shook his head.

'That's a swell spirit, Babe, but I wouldn't let you do that. You're my wife, an' it's up to me to support you. And that's the way it's goin' to be.' He rose and stretched. 'I got to go down and see about my licence. I'm goin' to be on the job, nine o'clock to-morrow mornin'.' He took up his hat and went to the door. 'We'll go to a show when I get back.'

Babe waited till she heard the lift door slam, and then took up the transmitter from the phone base. She called a Harlem number. After a minute the wire crackled back.

'Hello – that you, Gert? It's an old friend of yours – Babe. . . . That's right. Is Jenny there? Drunk? Well, if she ain't tell her to meet me around at Toni's back room in an hour. I'll tell you all about myself when I come up with Jenny. Sure I will.'

12

◆◇◆

BABE LEARNS A NEW RACKET

WITHIN an hour after she had called Nigger Gert's, Babe was in Toni's back room. Toni was out, but Henry, the giant bartender, greeted her effusively and set her up to the best he had in the place.

'Sure glad to see you, Miss Gordon,' he said.

Babe gave him a dazzling smile.

'Glad to see you, Henry. How's things with Toni?'

'Lively, Miss Gordon. Plenty of goin's on. You been missin' a lot by not bein' around here nights.'

There was a rap on the side door. Henry looked through the peek and opened the door to Jenny. Cokey was dolled up in a flowery dress with a streaming bow in the back, flesh stockings, patent-leather shoes and black picture hat. A belligerent smile curled at the corners of her lips and cold hate flared in steel eyes, as she confronted Babe.

'Hello, Jenny,' Babe greeted her. 'Say, don't you look like Small's all lit up? Must have hit the numbers or cleaned up on the Derby. Anyway, looks like Alec, the Greek florist, is keeping you in clothes from the look of that dress.'

'The hell you say!' Cokey Jenny jabbed a doubled-up fist against her lips. 'Well, they ain't no ham prizefighter's last shirt. If I got clothes it's from guys that can afford to pay for 'em.'

'You've always been very particular how you picked up your cash, ain't you, Jenny?' Babe said with a laugh.

'Never made a laugh of myself the way you done. And you high-hattin' me 'cause you got respectable and married. I'm not good enough for you no more.'

'I couldn't help it, Jenny – not seein' you – because Charlie wouldn't let us see anyone uptown till after the big fight was over. Honest, Jen, I missed you awful. I wanted to see you, but Charlie and the Bearcat was always around and I couldn't get away. Charlie put the knocks in against me with the Bearcat. I been tryin' to get you on the phone for weeks.' Of course, Babe was lying with her usual ease. 'Oh, listen, Jen, I got a lot of new things, and I picked out two dresses and a coat that will look great on you with a little fixing.'

Babe had found the way to her old pal's heart. Jenny softened when she heard about the dresses.

'Yeah?' she said interestedly. 'Ya mean that, Babe?'

'Don't mean nothin' else,' Babe answered. 'But, gee, it's good to see you, kid, and you look swell too. Honest, our separatin' has been a blessin' for you. Look at you. Must be a hostess in some chop suey dance hall.'

Jenny grinned.

'The Pavillion. I got the cigarettes there.'

'Yeah?' Babe appeared to be astonished.

'Harry and Lou put me up there. They often speak of you, Babe, and your swell parties. Must have had some snow around.'

'What are you drinkin', Jen?' Babe inquired. She thought: 'I've got to find out about this business with Harry and Lou. There may be something doing for me.'

'I'll take rye,' Jenny replied to Babe's question.

Babe turned to the bartender.

'Gimme a half-pint of rye, Henry.'

'Yes, Miss Gordon.' Henry reached down under the bar and stood the requested half-pint on the polished top.

Babe drew the cork and filled a glass for Jenny.

'Ain't playin' the Marathon no more, are you, Jen?'

Jenny tossed off the straight drink and then blew out a mouthful of whisky-laden breath.

'Don't have to wit' Lou and Harry lookin' after me. They got a big proposition for me. Some new racket about handlin' the stuff. Nothin' but big dough in it. Eveythin' percentage. I'll be makin' plenty.'

Babe was intensely interested.

'Maybe with what you make and what I get from the Bearcat we can start a place of our own up here.'

Cokey Jenny smiled her approval of the idea as she refilled her glass.

'Yeah. A swell trade trick house, maybe?'

'Nothin' but.'

Jenny gulped down he liquor and filled the glass up again to the brim. That finished the half-pint, and she looked at the empty bottle with regret.

'I got to be goin', Babe,' she said. 'Harry's expectin' me at the Pavillion.'

'Well, so long, Jenny. I'll be seein' you right along now.'

'So long, Babe.' The door closed after Jenny's streaming bow.

Babe smiled to herself. 'The sap,' she thought. She went to the pay telephone that hung on the wall, and, placing her mouth very close to the receiver called the Pavillion. She asked if she could talk to Harry, said it was on business, and that she was phoning from Toni's. Almost immediately she heard Harry's cigarette cough over the phone.

'Hello,' he coughed.

'Harry?'

'Well?' he inquired cautiously.

'Babe – Babe Gordon.'

'Well, for the love of Mike! What are you doing at Toni's at five-thirty in the afternoon?'

'Just popped in; thought I might see you here,' Babe informed him. 'But I met Jenny and she told me where to reach you.'

'How's things?'

'Not so good. Oh, I got somethin' important to tell you. Somethin' you ought to know. Get me?'

'I guess so,' Harry said. 'When can I see you?'

'Well, you'll have to make it right away, because I have to get back downtown to meet the Bearcat. Where's Lou?'

'Right here,' said Harry 'Listen, me and Lou will hop right over.'

Babe went inside and sat at a table in a corner. In a quarter of an hour Lou and Harry came in from the bar. They sat down with Babe.

Harry hung a cigarette on his lower lip and said:

'Hello, Babe. Quittin' the Bearcat?'

Babe held her cigarette to the flame he offered her.

'Not this minute, but he's all washed up fighting. Charlie bounced him. Driving a taxi, startin' to-morrow. And he expects me to stick.'

Harry smiled cynically. And Lou asked:

'Are you?'

Babe bunched her mouth in an expression of distaste. Then she tapped the ash from her cigarette with a slender, well-kept forefinger.

'What are you offerin' Jenny?' she shot at them.

Lou looked startled. Harry's eyelids drooped and there came a cruel glint from under them.

'What did she say?' said Harry slowly.

Babe took a deep inhale and let the smoke drift gently through her nostrils. Her tone was casual.

'Oh, she told me you had her workin' up in the Pavillion and had a big percentage job for her that'll pay her plenty. You know Jenny. She was drinkin' and shootin' off her mouth around here about it.'

Harry's look was that of a killer as he turned to Lou.

'What did I tell you, Lou? She can't keep her pan closed. It's suicide to put anybody in there like Cokey.'

Lou grunted.

'What's the matter with givin' me a break? How about lettin' me in on somethin' good?' said Babe.

Harry placed his hand on Lou's arm. Lou nodded his head.

'What is it?' Babe asked.

Lou rose and jerked his thumb toward the door. Harry paid the bill and the three patrons left Toni's. They got into Lou's car.

The latter was at the wheel and Harry climbed in the back after Babe. He took a rod from the side-pocket of his coat and slid it into the holster under his left armpit. Harry's business was a dangerous one; he was always prepared for any eventuality. He lit a cigarette as the car pulled away from the kerb. Then he bent close to Babe so that her ear was close to his mouth.

'We're fixin' to go into a five and ten cent store up here, with these.' He drew a small carton out of his inside pocket. It looked like a cigarette tin. Babe took it and removed the cover. There were a dozen gold-plated rouge compacts in the box. The chalk-rouge lifted out, and in the cavity were four three-and-a-half-grain cubes of morphine.

'Ten dollars apiece,' Harry said, 'and a hundred for the carton. We were figurin' on Jenny, but there ain't nobody was made for the job like you, Babe. You were born for it.'

Babe didn't hesitate a second.

'All right,' she said crisply, 'what's my rake-off?'

'One-third on everything. Morphine, heroin, and coke. Is it a go?'

'Sure. When?'

'We'll talk it over to-morrow up at the Club Sugar Cane. We'll know definitely then. How's that?'

'Okay with me.'

Harry leaned forward in his seat.

'Babe's willin' to come in with us,' he told Lou. 'That all right?'

'Sure,' Lou said over his shoulder. 'We can't miss with her.'

They were at 125th Street and Seventh Avenue.

'Let me off here,' said Babe. 'I'll cab from here.'

The car pulled in at the kerb.

Spanish Harry helped her out.

'Make it ten o'clock to-morrow at Toni's,' he said in parting. 'From there we'll jump over to the Club Sugar Cane.'

She returned to the hotel. The Bearcat came in a few minutes later. He had his licence, his taxi, and was ready to begin his new work the next day. He did not know that Babe, too, was ready to begin her new job, or that she had been uptown seeing Jenny and the old crowd. They went out to dinner at a nearby restaurant and then took a walk in Central Park. And at ten o'clock the Bearcat was in bed. Babe lay awake a long time, her mind busy with plans.

13

'TAXI'

THE next day, the Bearcat began his life as a taxi driver. He commenced to get a close-up of human nature that had formerly been hidden from him through his preoccupation with the fight game and Babe.

He had many fares his first day, which impressed him because he hadn't expected to be hailed by such an array of strangers. He picked up his third fare shortly before noon. It was a middle-aged woman, extremely well dressed, with quite motherly features. As he drove her toward the address she had given him, she conversed with him.

'You taxi-drivers must have an interesting life,' she said. 'You see so many different kinds of people. People always fascinate me. I like to imagine what they're thinking about. Don't you?' She leaned forward expectantly.

'Well, to tell you the truth, lady,' the Bearcat replied, 'this is my first day as a taxi-driver. I can't tell yet how interestin' it's goin' to be.'

'Your first day?' she went on. 'My, my – then you have a lot to learn. I notice you have a mirror up in front there. Can't you see me? I can see you.'

'Yeah,' said the Bearcat, wondering what this was all about. 'I can see you in it.'

'Well, you know,' she giggled, 'experienced taxi-drivers

remove their mirrors. Especially those that drive at night. I would advise you, if you drive at night, to take it down.'

'What for, lady?' the Bearcat inquired curiously.

'Well, because lovers who ride in cabs don't like to have the driver watching them, you know.'

The Bearcat laughed.

'Gee, I never thought of that!' He thought about when he and Babe had ridden in cabs, and wondered if the drivers had watched them. He smiled at the idea.

'Cabs are often turned down on account of those mirrors,' the lady gushed on. 'So this is your first day. Let me see if I can guess what you did before.' She leaned forward in her seat and looked at the Bearcat's profile. 'I think that you have been a prizefighter.'

'That's right,' the Bearcat said. 'That's what I was.'

The woman gave a little laugh.

'There – you see. I can read people. A prizefighter. Oh, it must be marvellous to have such a wonderful physique.'

'What's that?' the Bearcat inquired.

'I say it must be marvellous to have such a wonderful physique.'

'Oh,' said the Bearcat.

'So strong and everything. I love strong, healthy men. They're the salvation of our race.'

'Yeah?' said the Bearcat, as he slid the car up to the kerb before the address she had told him. He sprang out, opened the door and assisted her out. She gave him a playful smile.

He handed her the change, and she gave him a dollar tip. As he took it from her with grateful thanks, her hand closed on his.

'Wouldn't you like to come up and have a cooling drink?' she said. 'It's so warm to-day.'

'No, thanks, lady,' the Bearcat said. 'I got to keep on the go, if I want to make any money.'

'Oh,' she said almost pleadingly, 'you wouldn't be wasting your time, you know. I should enjoy your company, and I'd be glad to make it worth your while.'

'I'm sorry, lady.'

'Say, if we made it ten dollars.'

'Oh, thanks, lady. But I couldn't. I'd like to. If you want to make it some other time, I'd be glad to come up.'

'Very well then,' she said. 'It's a promise. You'll remember the address and I'm in apartment seven.'

The Bearcat had no intention of seeing her again. He was a little afraid of the woman. So strange! 'She must be a little nuts,' he thought. After a week or two more of taxi-driving perhaps he would understand.

About the middle of the afternoon he had another call that attracted his attention. A distinguished-looking tall man, with snow-white hair and well-groomed body, got into the cab with a woman who was highly rouged and expensively attired from shoes to the beautiful summer furs about her shoulders. He caught snatches of their conversation.

'But I don't want to stop at the Plaza for tea,' the man was saying irritably. 'You just want to show off that new fur I bought you.'

'Please, honey,' the girl begged.

'No, no. I'd be bored stiff. Let's go up to the apartment.'

'But I don't want to go up there yet. It's too early.'

'What has the time got to do with it? We can't get anything to drink at the Plaza.'

The girl's voice grew loud and harsh.

'You're afraid you'll meet some of your high-hat friends there. You're ashamed of me!'

'Please, please,' the man begged, 'don't shout in my ear. And how many times have I told you to speak quietly and not shriek like a London fishmonger.'

The girl started to cry. It sounded fake to the Bearcat.

'There you go callin' me names again,' the girl sobbed.

'Good lord! I'm not calling you names. Don't be silly. And stop sniffling. People are looking in at us.'

The crying stopped immediately.

'All right, then,' the girl said. 'If you don't take me to the Plaza, I won't be nice to you the way you like, any more.'

'Oh, I say now, Zelda,' the man argued. 'That's not sporting, after I've given you so much.'

'Well, I don't care,' said the girl. 'I just won't be nice that way any more, that's all.'

'Oh, good lord!' the man exclaimed anxiously. 'Well, all right.' He rapped on the taxi window with his stick. 'I say, my man.'

'Yeah?' the Bearcat answered as he choked down the speed of the car.

'Drive us to the Plaza – the Plaza!'

'Oh, you darling!' cried the girl.

'Be careful,' said the man. 'Confound it! Look, you've got powder all over my shoulder.'

The Bearcat scratched his head in wonder when they had entered the hotel. The man had tipped him fifteen cents. The clock had recorded two dollars and a quarter. Expensive furs, the Plaza for tea, and a lousy fifteen cents.

As he swung back along Fifth Avenue, going downtown, he was hailed and two men got in. They were sporty-looking guys, with quick-darting furtive eyes, and thin cruel lips.

'Go over the Queensborough Bridge and out along Queens Boulevard till we tell you to stop.' They lit cigarettes and settled back in the car. It was growing dark.

Some of their talk – strange, sinister – came faintly to the Bearcat.

'Got word that they're gonna spring Dapper to-night,' said one.

'Yeah. He's been in the big house for six months.'

'They got a screw fixed up there. After we do the business to-night, he'll get a tip-off that everything's okay.'

'What's he gonna do when we get word to the hideaway?'

'Dapper's goin' to Chicago. Chip and Bottlehead are drivin' him to Cleveland, where they'll make a connection for him to be taken the rest of the way. I'm followin' him to-morrow night.'

'What about me?'

'You'll cover this end. All you got to do is stay solid. If they dog you, call up the mouthpiece, see?'

The Bearcat was driving them along a stretch of Queens Boulevard lined on both sides by vacant lots overgrown with weeds and shrubbery. Pulled up, off to one side of the road, was a touring car with curtains fastened down.

'Stop here!' ordered the man who seemed to be the leader of the two.

'That must be Bottlehead waitin',' said the other as they got out of the cab.

The leader shoved five dollars into the Bearcat's hand.

'Keep it,' he said. 'But you ain't seen us – you ain't never goin' to remember us if you see us again, see. Be a wise guy and don't forget that, an' you'll stay healthy. Otherwise . . . ' His hand in his coat-pocket shoved forward. It gripped some pointed instrument.

The Bearcat felt no fear. He was only annoyed to think that they could bulldoze him. He felt like taking a poke at them. But he had more than his fare, so why butt into their game?

'I ain't interested in you,' said the Bearcat.

'Well, now, you're bein' smart,' said the man who held his hand in his pocket. 'And don't bother rememberin' the number of that car over there, either.'

'Okay,' said the Bearcat.

The man ran across the road to the car, which had its motor running. They jumped in and started of at a terrific speed.

And so the Bearcat found a taxi to be a cross-section of humanity, a world in itself.

14

BABE STEPS OUT

BABE kept her promise and met Lou and Harry at Toni's the next morning at ten o'clock. The three went from there to the Sugar Cane Club where they could discuss business without interruption during the morning hours. Lou explained that there was a salesgirl in the store where they wanted Babe to work who would let them know when a job was open, then the girl would take Babe to the manager and introduce her as a friend and room-mate. It would be up to Babe to get the job without arousing any suspicion. However, they particularly wanted Babe to be at the cosmetic counter, for there she could dispose of the dope-filled rouge compacts without attracting attention.

This meant that Babe might have to wait several weeks before she could begin work, but Lou and Harry were willing to wait until their agents could be planted right, for the dope racket brought in big profits.

While waiting for her new job Babe managed to have a good time even if the Bearcat did get on her nerves. She went out a lot at nights, as the Bearcat had changed his working shift. He found it much more profitable to operate his cab in the evening, because more money could be made in the late hours from the theatre crowds and night-club rounders. He did not return home before five in the morning, and sometimes later when his last call was a long one.

Babe managed to get home regularly before Bearcat arrived, but she knew sooner or later she was bound to overplay her hand. On a Sunday morning at the end of two weeks' waiting for her job Babe was caught. When the Bearcat returned to the hotel at five o'clock in the morning he found Babe out and saw that the bed had not been slept in. That worried him. He did not undress but sat in a chair by the window. The cheap alarm-clock he had bought showed five-thirty when Babe opened the door of their room.

The Bearcat sprang out of his chair. His face flushed with anger.

'So this is whatcha doin'. So this is why you wanted me to change my shift! Work nights instead of daytime, so you can go steppin' around!'

Babe stiffened. Then she threw her wrap violently over the foot of the bed.

'Who's steppin' around? Where d'you get that steppin' around stuff?'

As she leaned toward him he got a whiff of her whisky breath.

'This is a fine way to come home to me.'

Babe stared back at him.

'Why, you're lucky I came home at all!'

The Bearcat grabbed hold of her.

'Who's the guy you was with?' he said through clenched teeth. 'Tell me, do you hear?' He shook her; jealous thoughts took possession of his mind. She must have been with some man. What else could keep her out to this hour but some guy?

'Tell me who he is, an' I'll kick his head off!'

He shook her.

'Where was you? Who is he? I'll go nuts if you don't tell me.'

She sobered up. She had never seen him act that way

before. His fingers dug into her arms. He did not mean to use his strength on her, but his frenzy got the better of him. He didn't realize what he was doing.

Babe tried to free herself.

'What man? There wasn't no man. There ain't no other man!'

'Don't tell me there wasn't. I know it – I feel it. All night I felt there was somethin' wrong. Damn you – tell me before I —'

He lifted her and threw her on the bed.

Babe managed to hold her temper and say: 'I tell you there was no one. If you'd only give me a chance to explain.'

She was half scared. He had a wild look in his eyes.

'Tell me, tell me! Where was you?' shouted Bearcat as he leaned over the bed.

She was sober enough now to make up a convincing story. She admitted having been up in Harlem. She couldn't think of another place quickly enough.

'I met Cokey Jenny. She felt bad 'cause I high-hatted her. She's been sick. We had a couple of drinks. A couple more girls came in and we had a few more. There wasn't a man in the place. I swear I haven't looked at another man in months. I know I did wrong, dear, drinkin' like this – I'm sorry. But I felt bad to-night and thought a couple of drinks would cheer me up.' Babe squeezed out a few tears.

She put her hand on her arm where his fingers had left red marks. The Bearcat softened. He felt that he had been a brute. He took her in his arms and kissed the bruises.

'I'm sorry, dear, I got so rough, but I just can't stand the idea of your steppin' out with some other guy.' He undressed her gently. After that she felt easier and less afraid. She was drowsy now the booze was wearing off and wanted to go to sleep if he would let her.

She got a new kick out of the Bearcat that night. The force of his emotions, his jealousy, gave her an unexpected thrill.

But she rapidly grew tired of his jealous outbursts whenever he arrived home first, and explanations became more and more difficult. She had to keep in touch with Lou and Harry about her prospective position. The matter could not safely be discussed over the telephone, so she frequented the Harlem night clubs. She haunted Sonnie's, Small's Paradise, The Net, Barron's, the Hotsy Club, with Sunday night highlights at the Harlem Breakfast Club.

Then one night Harry passed her the word that she was to go into Baldwin's Five and Ten Cent store the next day and apply for the job that was open behind the cosmetic counter. Having landed the job Babe decided she was through with married life.

The Bearcat, coming into the hotel room at five the following morning, saw she was not there.

'Babe!' he called, thinking she might have stepped into the bath. There was no answer. 'Where the hell is she?' he muttered as he looked around the room.

From the dressing-table there were several toilet articles missing. The wardrobe door stood open. The racks were empty. Her trunk was gone.

His face blanched. He knotted his hands and sat down on the bed to think, numb with apprehension. For the few moments required to regain any sense of reality he was submerged in a wave of self-pity, then as the blood rushed back to his head he saw red.

Leaping to the telephone he snapped off the receiver.

'Did Mrs. Delaney leave any message when she went out?' he asked the switchboard operator.

'No, sir. She did not,' replied the clerk.

The Bearcat hung up. He rushed out and rang for the lift. When it came up he said to the lift boy:

'Did you see Mrs. Delaney go out?'

'Yas, suh,' said the coloured boy.

'When?'

''Bout two hours ago.'

'Do you know where she went?'

'Ah do' know, boss. She jus' gone, da's all. Ah know Ah took her down in duh elevator an' put her grip in a taxi. She didn't say nothing.'

'What kind of a taxi was it? One that stands in front of the hotel?'

'No, suh. Jus' a taxi comin' along. Jus' a pick-up taxi.'

'Who took her trunk down?'

'Duh po'ter done took it down in duh fweight elevator an' put it in duh cab.'

'Where is the porter?'

'Downstairs, suh. Ah'll send him up to yo' ef yo' wants me to.'

'All right, send him up and be quick about it.'

'Suhtainly, boss. Ah'm sorry Ah can't help yo'. She jus' gimme a half-dollar an' go, da's all.'

The Bearcat slipped the boy a quarter and returned to his room pacing up and down until the porter entered.

'When you took Mrs. Delaney's trunk and put it in the cab, did you hear her tell the driver where to take her?'

'No, suh,' said the porter. 'Ah jus' knows she gimme a quarter, an' Ah went away fum dere. Ah'd sho tell yo' ef Ah knew anythin'.'

The Bearcat also rewarded this person with a quarter, and sent him away. He seized his hat, ran to his garage, got his taxi and searched Harlem. It was a night of torture for him. He did not find a trace of her.

He couldn't eat or sleep for days. He called up all his friends and inquired about Babe, trying to learn of her whereabouts. He was rigid from fatigue and pain.

It was over a week before he located Babe. He found her in a night club and dragged her out. He carried on so terribly in public that she got into his cab and returned to the hotel with him for the night. After hours of bitter quarrelling she admitted to him that she was working in the Baldwin Five and Ten. He tried to persuade her to leave her position. He didn't think it right for his wife to work.

She threatened to divorce him and absolutely refused to live with him. The next day she was afraid he might show up at the store and make trouble for her with the management. They wouldn't stand for any scandal. She must be rid of him or he might spoil her racket. At last she thought of a plan to get the Bearcat out of the way.

She looked up Joe Malone at his hotel. He was surprised to see her and gave her a warm welcome. She took a seat opposite Joe and lamped him with an appealing expression.

'Joe,' she began, 'I know you been a pal to me and the Bearcat and we think a lot of you. Now I want you to do somethin' for me. The Bearcat is gettin' terrible. I took a job up here in a Five and Ten to help him out, 'cause you know things went bad for us. He's been runnin' me ragged. He's gettin' jealous ideas, accusin' me of being around with guys. His own common sense ought to tell him if I was out for that sort of business I wouldn't be workin' back of a counter in a Five and Ten. If I happen to go in to take a drink with some of my friends, I don't know what minute he's comin' into drag me out and make a big scene. I just can't stand it any longer, Joe. It's bad for him. He's gettin' to be a nervous wreck. Says he can't sleep or eat any more, worryin'. I just had to leave him 'cause he's going nuts.'

Joe rubbed his chin.

'Yeah,' he said. 'I heard you wasn't livin' together. You know how quick them things git around.'

Babe nodded.

'Course it's silly for him to carry on like this when I ain't doin' anythin' wrong. He's just disgracin' me with all my friends, Joe.'

Joe had a sort of sympathetic look.

Babe saw this look and figured now was the time to work on him.

'Tell you what I want you to do for me, Joe. You're the only one I know can do this. I want you to talk to him and show him where he's all wrong. See if you can't get him into goin' away to some camp for his nerves. Start him back to trainin'. I think if he tries hard enough he can make a comeback. Then he an' I can be happy again. I got enough money saved for the trip. But the thing is, if he knew it came from me he wouldn't take it. You know he's got old-fashioned ideas about takin' money from women. So if you'll go an' tell him that you'll loan him the money . . . '

'Sure, Babe,' Joe said. 'I'll take him up to the Adirondacks. I'm goin' up there. Been goin' up for the last five years. I'll tell you what I'll do. I'll go right over and see Bearcat now. I know where he parks.'

Babe took out a roll of bills and thrust them into Joe's willing hands.

'Joe,' she said, 'you don't know how much I appreciate this.'

Babe then proceeded uptown, and Joe headed for the Bearcat whose stand was in front of a nearby hotel. Joe found him working on the motor of his cab.

'Hello, Bearcat,' said Joe, emphasizing his greetings with a resounding slap on the back.

The Bearcat straightened up from his work and thrust out a grimy hand. 'Hello,' he said. 'Glad to see you.'

'I want to talk to you a minute,' Joe said. 'I just saw Babe and had a long talk wit' her. She's all broke up an' worried about you.'

The Bearcat gave a grunt of disdain.

'Worried about me? She won't even see me. What did she have to say? Tell me. She don't care a damn what happens to me. Who was with her? Who's the guy she's got? What she say?'

Joe stopped him with an upraised hand.

'Wait a minute! Say – you're all shot to pieces! Take it

easy. I'm tellin' you there ain't no other guy, Bearcat. The kid's on the level. Any dame that'll go an' stand behind a counter in a Five an' Ten like she's doin' has got plenty of guts an' nerve. I felt rotten when I heard she was workin' like that. An' she looked worried too. She's worryin' about you, Bearcat.'

'Then what did she leave me for?' the Bearcat demanded to know. 'I never looked at another skirt.'

'Well, women is funny sometimes like that,' Joe said wisely. 'They make sacrifices for a guy they fall for. I t'ink she felt she was doin' you no good. She was holdin' you back. She sorter hinted that maybe Charlie was right when he kicked about you bein' wit' her. She t'ought if she got away from you, it'd give you a chance to make a comeback.'

The Bearcat shook his head.

'Me make a comeback without her? Never. I tell you, Joe, I'm goin' nuts if I don't see her.' The Bearcat trembled, nervously trying to light a cigarette. 'Look at me, Joe. Can't even light a cigarette. A wonder I don't smash into somethin' drivin' this boat. Maybe I'd be better off if I did. Sometimes I feel like drivin' into a stone wall and finishin' it all.'

'I know how you feel,' Joe said soothingly, 'an' you got to snap out of it. You an' me is goin' to a training camp. You're gonna make a comeback.'

The Bearcat's eyes brightened for a moment at the idea and then became dull and despondent again.

'What's the use? Nothin' means anythin' to me now, Joe, without her.'

Joe placed his hand on the Bearcat's arm.

'You love the woman an' you want her back, don'tcha? There's only one way to get her, an' that's for you to show her what you're made of. You'll be back in the money in no time and buyin' her nice things again.'

'Maybe that's all she ever wanted me for.'

Joe shook his head.

'No, you got her wrong. She said she can't stand to see you workin' so hard for a few dollars to take her out when you go without things you need. That's why she's up behind that counter in the Five and Ten. Don't that prove that she loves you?'

'It sounds funny to me,' said the Bearcat.

'Didn't I tell you women is queer that way?'

The Bearcat stared into space with a bewildered look trying to figure it out. He wanted to believe Joe.

'I'll be on the up an' up with you, Bearcat,' Joe told him. 'I'll tell you the truth. She begged me to take you away. The girl acshally cried. I seen the tears in her eyes mesef. You got to go. This is your only chance. The only way to make her happy.'

The Bearcat stuck out his hand.

'Joe, you always was a friend in need.'

Joe grinned.

The next day Bearcat rented his taxi on a percentage basis, bought some gym clothes and met Joe on the Albany boat *en route* for the training camp in the Adirondacks.

Joe saw that the good word reached Babe. She was free now to continue in the dope racket without fear of Bearcat's busting up the game. And what a choice line of customers came regularly for rouge sticks! Her end of the profits mounted up. Then too the guys that came to her apartment paid well.

15

HARLEM

THE old, old story of civilization's lusts was being retold in Harlem. The lusts that ancient Rome and Athens could not purge from their proud and disciplined cultures – the flesh cry that has persisted through all time – found expression and release in the region of New York's black belt.

Harlem is the Paris of the Western Hemisphere – a museum of occult sex, a sensual oasis in the sterile desert of white civilization, where conventional people can indulge in unconventional excesses.

In Harlem the hell-holes flourish side by side with high-coloured respectability. A house of prostitution secretly carries on its traffic next to a church. Abominations are offered for sale so guardedly that even the most observant cannot guess what is going on. In yesteryears Chicago and New York's Chinatown were the oases for those seeking sensual diversions or perversions. Now Harlem is the pool of sex, where all colours are blended, all bloods mingled. A pool whose overflow will colour the mind and body of countless thousands for generations to come.

Breathing this atmosphere, Babe was in her element. In another incarnation she might have been a votary of Aphrodite, sitting in the temple gardens with her face lightly veiled to the eyes.

Babe had been one man's woman too long to hanker for the diversified gluttonies of her street days with Cokey Jenny. The excitement that a constant stream of men roused in her sensual temperament was afforded by the adventure of the dope racket she was in. The man-hunt was no longer an economic necessity, as she was making big money with Lou and Harry. Selling dope gave her a great kick, an absolutely new kind of power. The risks of detection only added glamour to the game.

Babe had plenty of new clothes and a very attractive apartment of her own in Washington Heights. After her day's work in Baldwin's Five and Ten was done, she spent the early evening resting at home, then at midnight she flung herself into the gay, carefree night life of Harlem.

She had to be in at work at nine o'clock every morning, but she managed to get along on a few hours' sleep at night, just as thousands of other girls in New York City do.

She went everywhere – sometimes in the company of Lou and Harry, often with Money Johnson as her escort. They would join mixed colour parties going from one place to another, drinking and dancing, with sex always beguiling them on to madder music or more sensuous scenes.

On her pleasure rounds Babe saw many blasé white society women gaily dancing with men of every shade of colour from the cream of the creole to the charcoal black of darkest Africa – negro girls with soft brown eyes and fertile bodies filled with primitive fire, sitting with their white lovers, happy to be seen with men of social standing, wealth, and culture.

Near the club rooms of the Negro Vaudeville Artists' Association were the 'circuses' or 'peep-shows' where, if one had the price, one could watch the antics of blacks.

This was the hectic underworld of Harlem that Babe knew so well. And even this was only a veiled glimpse of the unmentionable things it offered for a price.

Babe had long been acquainted with an infinite variety of diversions. After the dull routine of her married life she came back to her fancy work with fresh enjoyment.

One of Babe's favourite night resorts was the Harlem Breakfast Club. It got the 'breakfast' part of its name because it opened at midnight and closed at midday, which pretty well covered the breakfast hour of its patrons. She loved it because it had more swank than most of the other places. There was always a white society crowd there, and the music, cabaret, and general atmosphere were all bound to be hotter than hot.

It was here that Wayne Baldwin, Jr., first saw Babe Gordon. He had recently returned from Paris where he was surprised and mildly shocked by the freedom with which whites and blacks fraternized. One night he was discussing the matter at his club when Jack Rathburne exclaimed:

'Good Lord! Don't you know that right in Harlem you can see more mixing of white and black in one night than you can see in a month in Paris?'

Baldwin was a bit sceptical. He admitted he had never been to Harlem except to visit their local store, but was willing to be shown. He was the son of W. W. Baldwin, founder of the great chain of Five and Ten Cent stores bearing his name. Wayne was now sales-manager of the company and a frequent visitor to all their more important branches.

Rathburne as an habitué of Harlem made up a party to show Baldwin the sights. Leonard Colton and Barry Washburn went along with them. These four young men were Social Registerites and looked every inch of it. Wayne Baldwin was by far the outstanding figure. He was tall, slender, with a fine breadth of shoulders. His evening clothes, made in Bond Street, seemed as much a part of him as his dark wavy hair. He possessed that illusive quality called 'charm'.

Rathburne naturally appointed himself official guide of the party. He piloted them to all the well-known resorts, reserving the Harlem Breakfast Club as a climax to the evening.

Everywhere they went they drank freely, so that when they finally arrived at the Harlem they were just in the right mood for sport.

'This is the maddest place in town,' Rathburne said, as an obsequious waiter showed them to a table on the rim of the dance floor. 'Wayne, prepare to hear your Puritanical ancestors turning over in their graves to-night.'

They all laughed.

'If you expect me to be shocked to death, Jack,' said Baldwin, 'you'll be disappointed. I disowned my ancestors long ago. There were too many pirates in the crowd.'

The others roared at that, the liquor they had consumed made the remark seem all the more pungent.

'Good boy!' said Leonard Colton. 'Let's have another drink.'

'Well,' said Jack, 'all I've got to say is, don't tell Alice I dragged you in here.'

Alice was Baldwin's sister. She and rollicking Jack Rathburne had reached the point where all that was needed was an engagement ring.

'Don't worry,' said Baldwin. 'I won't. Alice has high-hatted me ever since I came home from Paris. She's been kind of hinting around, digging at me with odd questions. I think she's dying to know whether I had a string of mistresses while I was abroad. I wonder you don't find Alice too strait-laced, Jack. You know you'll have to cut out this sort of thing if you marry that precious sister of mine.'

Jack sighed. 'I suppose I'll have to. But she's worth it.'

Barry Washburn placed his hand on Baldwin's arm, and leaning over to the others said in a low voice:

'Say, listen in on the next table.'

They sipped their drinks slowly with ears alert.

At the next table was a high yellow, a big boudoir man with lust in his eyes, loving up three brown-skinned women who were going after him in a big way.

'Ah sure want yo' hot stuff. When yo' goin' to commit grand fo' me?' said one of the girls.

'Hush up. No yaller gal goin' to get me 'cept she's got two cars or mo'. Less'n dat Ah ain't enticed. Ah ain't even toleratin' yer.'

'That's the way to handle women, Wayne,' muttered Colton, with a laugh.

Baldwin gulped down his highball and ordered another round.

'These niggers are all alike. That kind of stuff is all they think about,' he caustically remarked to his friends.

Crowds began to flock into the Harlem Breakfast Club and by three o'clock the place had reached its highest pitch of excitement.

Hell . . . The inferno of sexual passion had broken loose!

16

ORGY

Y ES, hell had broken loose at the Harlem Breakfast Club! The coloured band was playing with its soul in every note. It had to play at fever pitch to bring out the cry of passion and debauch.

The bodies of almost naked coloured women, wriggling and squirming, moved about the dance floor; brown-skinned busts shook frenziedly, hips swayed, abdomens protruded. The music excited, irritated, inflamed the animal instincts.

Spotlights swept over a white and black checkerboard. At one table in a blinding calcium glare a society group had its eyes riveted on a black hula dancer, weaving sensuously up and down near the corner of their table. An elderly, ultra-fashionable woman in the party looked on scandalized and shocked, it being her first visit to Harlem. As her horror grew, the coloured girl increased her contortions. The crowd laughed and cheered, which assured the black dancer that her efforts to shock were being appreciated.

At the edge of the dance floor, Wayne Baldwin had a reserved table. He and his three friends were drunk, and thoroughly enjoying the orgy around them.

Baldwin's eyes fastened themselves on a gorgeous woman draped in white ermine. It was Babe Gordon. Ordinarily Baldwin would have glanced at her and said, 'A beautiful woman' – and thought nothing more. But here in this particular setting she flashed out like a white diamond. Was she unescorted, he wondered. There was no one at her table. He was anxious to know who she was. He couldn't help admiring her.

His friends called his attention back to another round of drinks. While he drank, the woman's beauty burned in his eyes. She was a sublime creature. One swallow of liquor and he looked back at her table.

Through his daze, he now saw a big grinning negro sitting close to her. He choked with horrified astonishment. Signalling a coloured waiter, he slipped him a dollar and asked:

'Who is that man with the white woman over there?'

'Why, boss,' said the waiter, 'that's Money Johnson. Dat boy got so much money he do' know which end to start spendin' it. All duh women jus' crazy 'bout him like he was duh Prince o' Wales.'

So the big coloured brute was Money Johnson.

Baldwin stared impolitely at them for several moments.

Money Johnson was a huge, lordly lion with plenty of self-assurance. His sunny features and hot burning eyes held a magnetism that irresistibly drew the attention of women to him. His magnificent body, lynx-eyes, and pearly-white grin had brought the women of Harlem crawling to him, hungering for even an affectionate glance.

A couple of years ago, Johnson was a kerbstone pimp sporting custom-built suits and barber-pole shirts because infatuated Harlem girls hustled for him and handed over their earnings for the thrill of his arm about their waists. Shop girls and waitresses turned over their week's pay to him, only too happy if he thought enough of them to accept it. With the cash they harvested for him, Johnson opened basement gin mills, took racing bets and banked a 'policy' game.

He cornered the business of playing the numbers in Harlem.

Cash poured on him in a steady green river until he was neck deep in it. To use his own expression, 'He was lousy with the filthy stuff.' Wherever he was seen he was taking or passing green-backs, so Harlem called him 'Money' Johnson.

Johnson lived like an emperor in highbrow Strivers' Row, Harlem's Park Avenue, with two cars and a chauffeur at the disposal of his mistresses. He had the pick of the dusky Harlem girls but no longer found coloured women attractive. He craved white women. He wanted the whitest and most beautiful, and so he fell for Babe Gordon.

Yes, Babe Gordon had a nigger lover. Why not? Other white women had them.

Baldwin continued to look at the dazzling woman sitting close to Money Johnson – a chain of diamonds about her throat, shimmering stones on her fingers and slender wrists. The arm of the coloured Apollo was over the back of Babe's chair, and his large, bronze hand rested on her ermine shoulders, the finger-tips caressing her cream-white throat. The saxophones crooned a low barbaric jungle moan. Baldwin looked on fascinated, unable to take his eyes off the monstrous sight that held him spellbound.

Could that woman be so blasé and jaded that she had to visit this jungle for thrills? He loathed her, yet desired her.

In spite of this instinctive antagonism toward the negro who was intruding into the forbidden circle of white caste, Baldwin was forced to admit that he was a magnificent animal.

He turned his eyes away in loathing from this public exhibition of sensual pleasure. He wanted to do something to shame the woman and put that burly dinge back in his place. His brain was spinning madly. 'Why, I could give her all that, if she'd let me. And that's what I want to be to her right now – her lover.'

The music grew more sensuous, vibrant with passion.

He rose dramatically from the table and, seizing his glass, sent it crashing to the floor.

Baldwin was just another early-morning drunk to the rest of the crowd in the cabaret. Only his own party, drunk like all the rest, looked astonished for a moment, wondering what had caused his sudden outburst. They laid it to the bad liquor, but tried to persuade him to sit down and have just one more drink. With balanced feet but unbalanced mind, Baldwin without a word of explanation suddenly stalked to the cloak-room, demanded his hat and stick, then disappeared into the murky night. The saxophones groaned on. The spotlights stabbed out in the dark like star-shells over No Man's Land. Drunken joy surged to the centre of the floor and barbarous urge led to a shouting ecstasy which ended only with exhaustion. Black bodies glistened and their pungent smell mingled with the fumes of raw whisky. Baldwin's party had seen, heard, and tasted enough, some of them too much, in one way or another, so they lurched to the street and their waiting car.

17

HIS OFAY BROAD

WHEN Baldwin made his sudden exit from the Harlem Breakfast Club, his friends merely thought he was drunk and needed some fresh air. They found him seated in the back of his car waiting for them.

He explained that the heat and drinks had gone to his head so he had hurried out to cool off. Amidst a good deal of drunken chaffing they were driven downtown and delivered to their respective homes by Baldwin's discreet chauffeur.

Meanwhile, at the club the orgy continued to rage, and it was not until seven o'clock in the morning that Babe Gordon and Money Johnson emerged from the club and got into the limousine that stood waiting for them at the kerb.

The big foreign car swung up Seventh Avenue on its way to Johnson's elaborate, gaudy apartment in Strivers' Row.

Walking along in the same direction as the car were two well-known dusky characters of Harlem's night life, on their way home to bed. One spoke with a high, squeaky voice and had a girlish laugh which partly explained his nickname of Madame Jolly. The other was Willie. Just Willie, known by no other name but easily identified by the pink silk handkerchief always carried in his sleeve. These two knew everything about who's who and what's what and that's that in Harlem.

Madame Jolly was the first one to spot Babe and Money Johnson in the car as it purred by them.

'Lan', chile,' he cried to Willie, 'did yo' see dat? Dere goes Money Johnson wit' his ofay broad. Beautiful gal! Sweet Mama! Lor', chile, he ain't dealin' in nothin' now but pink-toes!'

Willie's eyes bulged in his head.

'Look at 'im bustin' up duh avenyer! Mm! Mm!'

'Better not let pretty Marie see him,' said Madame Jolly. 'She don' stand aside fo' none o' dem blondes. Chile, ef she catch him she gonna kick him so hard dey'll have to take him to duh Hospital to pull her foot out!'

Willie grinned.

'Ah hears all duh yalla gals jus' 'bout goin' crazy since Money gone pink-chasin'! Tell me he livin' lak a king up dere in Strivers' Row in a palacious apartment.'

Madame Jolly threw up his head.

'Lak a king? Lan', chile, yo' means like a emperorer, nothin' less.'

Willie nodded his head.

'Ah years he's got a gol' bed up dere, wit' steps roun' it. Yo' got to walk upstairs to git to bed.'

Madame Jolly rolled his eyes.

'Willie, don' Ah know, don' Ah know? Ah's been dere, Ah's been dere. He got a gol' bed up on a plate-form. An' lan', chile, he got silks an satins hangin' on duh walls, an' carpets on duh floor dat yo'd lak to sink in up to yo' knees; an' what dey calls duh sunken baftub right in duh floor. Yo' got to go downstairs to duh baftub an' upstairs to duh bed. An' lan', chile, he got pitchers ob naked women all over duh place. Dere's one pitcher ob a naked woman on a white horse wit' long yalla hair hangin' down.'

Willie looked startled.

'Duh white horse has got long yalla hair hangin' down?'

'No, fool man. Duh woman on duh horse has got yalla hair!'

'Mm, mm!' said Willie. 'Tell me mo'.'

'Lan', chile,' continued Madame Jolly, 'yo' ain't heard nothin'. We's up dere on a party one night an' dat high yalla Topaze, she lay in dat gorgeous gol' bed wit' silk sheets, an' she say to Money, 'Come on, baby, come ovah heah to yo' sweet mama'!'

Willie had an anxious look.

'What Money say? Chile, go on, dat ain't dirt, dat's mud. Dat's what yo' call ol' red clay fum down home. Go on, dish it, disher! What Money say to dat, huh? What Money say to Topaze?'

Madame Jolly gave vent to a shrill laugh.

'Lan', chile, Money jus' laugh at her. He say, 'Git up out o' dat bed, woman. Dat bed ain't meant fo' yo'. Any ol' cot good enough fo' yo' hide'!'

Willie roared.

'Ain't dat somepin! What Topaze say?'

'Lor', chile, she ain't say nothin', she jus' so mad, she jus' ravin'.'

'Tell me mo',' said Willie. 'Mah ears is leanin' at yo'.'

'Chile,' said Madame Jolly, 'yo'll stop breathin' when Ah tell yo' dis. Money got dat room where duh bed is all surrounded wit' lookin'-glasses. Lookin'-glasses on duh ceilin', lookin'-glasses on duh door, lookin'-glasses on duh four walls an' lookin'-glasses in duh floor. Ever'where yo' look yo' see yo'self a thousan' times. An' when he's in dat room Ah bet he see himself in 'em lookin'-glasses an' thinks he's a whole army. Willie, Ah'm tellin' yo', after Ah looked at mahself in dose lookin'-glasses fo' five minutes Ah never was so sick o' one person as me in all mah life. But dis new pink gal o' his ain't gonna have Money long ef Big Ida gist a-hold o' him. She just gonna snatch him bald-headed. He just gonna lak to die.'

Willie grinned in anticipation.

'Ah knows one t'ing: dat all dese here yalla gals Money

done threw down is gonna cut him up in little pieces when dey gets duh chance.'

'Lor', chile, don't fool yo'self. Dey all sure to come crawlin' back to him ef he hol' out his han'.'

Willie and Madame Jolly came to a corner and parted, shuffling their weary ways off to bed.

Yes, Money Johnson left a trail of broken hearts among the coloured women of Harlem. But what did he care as long as he had the most beautiful white woman a negro could ever dream of possessing?

He loved Babe with all his deep-rooted primitive passion. And she liked that passion. In that great mirrored room in Strivers' Row Money Johnson appeared like an army by reflection and she was like a shimmering white quicksand ready to consume these black battalions.

Wayne Baldwin was a busy young man, but in the two weeks that followed his first sight of Babe Gordon at the Harlem Breakfast Club he was unable to concentrate his attention on business duties. Whenever the vision of the black man and white woman flashed before his mind, which was frequently, he experienced the same violent emotions that he had known when they had been actually before him.

For the first time he voiced something of his feelings when he faced Jack Rathburne, his closest friend, across a dinner-table in the University Club. The meal invited confidences as they dallied over lighted cigarettes and demi-tasse.

'Jack,' said Baldwin. 'I've got something to tell you that is rather in the nature of a confession.'

'Good Lord!' said Jack laughingly. 'What have you been up to?'

'No,' said Baldwin, 'this is a serious matter, so until you hear what I have to say please don't make any comment.'

'All right, old man, I'm all attention,' answered Rathburne as he slowly sipped his coffee.

Baldwin tapped the ash from his cigarette and studied its lighted end for an instant.

'I didn't quite tell the truth,' he said, 'when I explained to you and the others about leaving the Harlem Breakfast Club so suddenly.'

Rathburne smiled.

'I thought you hadn't.'

Baldwin frowned as though lining up in his mind what he was going to say.

'I suppose when I tell you a woman was the cause of my diving out of the place, you'll make some stupid and cynical remark in bad French about *toujours la femme*.'

'Nothing was farther from my mind,' said Jack with a grin.

'Well, it was a woman. A beautiful woman. She was seated at a table in a corner of the room with a big negro, actually enjoying him, fascinated by him.'

'Do you mean that stunning blonde woman in an ermine wrap?' asked Rathburne. 'I did notice her, but I didn't see the negro.'

'Well, he came in later,' explained Baldwin. 'Come to think of it, you were at the opposite side of the table. Your back was to them. How in the name of all that's decent, Jack, could a woman like that, obviously a person of refinement, allow a black to make love to her?'

Jack crushed out his cigarette in a green-glass tray.

'A matter of taste, Wayne. In this case, a very depraved taste.'

'No, no,' said Baldwin. 'I can't believe that. There must be some other explanation. There must be some deeper motive than merely a bizarre attraction.'

Jack's face was serious.

'I think you've hit it there, Wayne.'

'What do you mean?'

116

'Bizarre attraction. In other words, *sexual preference*,' replied Jack.

'No. I can't believe it. Of course, I've seen plenty of white women with black men, and white men with black women, combinations that are undoubtedly the *result of sexual preference*. But this woman – well, I tell you, old man, she appeared different. It can't be that with her.'

Jack looked impatient.

'What else can it be?'

Baldwin drew another cigarette from his silver monogrammed case.

'That's just it, Jack. I don't know. But I'd like to find out.'

He lighted his cigarette with fingers that persisted in trembling.

Jack looked out of the window and then back to the quiet seclusion of the dining-room.

'Do you mean she's got under your skin? That you're really interested in her?'

'Yes,' said Baldwin – 'terribly.' His voice, too, was not quite under control.

This was a cropper.

They were silent for several minutes.

'If there is anything I can do, old boy, just say the word,' Jack finally said, for he somehow felt responsible for this mess.

'You'll think I'm crazy,' replied Wayne, 'but I've been up in Harlem every night since we were there together. I hoped I'd see her again; but she seems to have disappeared. You know a lot of people up there; perhaps they could tell you her whereabouts. Tell you her name.'

'You could have found out that night, if you'd only asked the waiter.'

'Oh, but I couldn't, Jack. I couldn't think of anything. My mind was in a whirl. It must have been the liquor that brought it on. It certainly got on my nerves to see a woman like that fascinated by a big negro. Well, anyway, I must know more about it. I must see her, yes, and talk with her.'

Rather ashamed at his vehemence, Wayne slumped down in his chair and then suddenly remembered a theatre engagement that just had to be kept.

'Well, I'm glad that's off my chest, Jack, and if you can help me find that goddess in ermine I'll be no end grateful. It's the only road back to sanity for me. So long; I'm really frightfully sorry that I have to abandon this conversation.'

After his friend had gone Jack wandered into the club library, and, sinking into a deep-dished leather chair, he murmured to himself over and over again, 'So Wayne has fallen for Babe Gordon.'

When Baldwin left the club he felt happier than he had for days. He was glad that he had told Jack. It was a relief to talk things over with someone who would understand.

As for Babe, she had not been seen around the night clubs for some time. Her time away from the store was spent in Money Johnson's apartment on Strivers' Row. She insisted that he throw elaborate parties there. The kind of parties she wanted ran into big money. She spun Johnson around her finger until he was dizzy.

Babe had to stay away from the store occasionally to catch up on sleep. Lou and Harry were afraid she would lose her job and so objected to Money Johnson. They told her that her affair with the black man was creating jealousy among Johnson's cast-off girl friends. They thought that one or another of these deserted and disappointed ladies might show up at the store and make no end of trouble, might in fact do some fast work with a razor. But Babe didn't care. Her life with Money Johnson satisfied her craving for excitement, and she was entirely without fear. Then something happened that changed everything.

Money Johnson, the 'policy king', was arrested on a gambling charge. After spending a wad of money and pulling political wires, he managed to have his sentence reduced to three months.

18

THE FRAME-UP

I N Nigger Gert's apartment in Harlem, a group of excited
chorus girls from the various coloured night clubs were
drinking 'corn' and lolling on the sofa and plush chairs as
they discussed in high-pitched tones the arrest and sentence
of Money Johnson.

Gert, who was passing out corn liquor, was a large, husky,
pitch black woman. She was busy between pouring and
answering the door-bell.

One tall, chocolate-skinned girl with close-cropped hair,
gold earrings, and red lacquered lips was pacing back and
forth in wild-eyed excitement, proclaiming dramatically with
spasmodic frenzied gestures. She thrust her finger at Nigger
Gert.

'Got jus' what was comin' to him, the lowdown dog. Ah
hope he rots in gaol. Ah tol' yo', Gert, sooner er later he'd
git his. Set me up another drink.'

Gert scowled.

'Listen, Topaze, yo' got to quit shoutin' lak dat or Ah ain't
goin' to serve yo' no mo' likker, yo' heah me?'

Topaze started off again.

'Ah don' care 'bout nothin' He done me dirt an' Ah'm glad
Ah fixed him. Ah wished the jedge had a-given him thirty
years, 'stead o' measly three months.'

One of the other girls interrupted with:

'Yo' was crazy to mess up wit' him in the firs' place. He never had no 'tention o' marryin' yo'!'

'Yes, he did!'

'Ah, hush up. Yo' jus' full o' dat stuff again, gal. Ah always tol' yo', yo' was a fool to git mix' up wit' him. An' Ah tol' yo' right, too di'n't Ah?'

'Goddam it!' Topaze turned venomously on the girl. 'Yo' don't know a damn thing 'bout it.'

The girl's eyes flashed back.

'How come ef Ah don't? Wasn't Ah in duh chorus an' yo' hostess at duh Savoy, when dat Money Johnson firs' come in duh place an' yo' begun makin' a fool o' yo'self, throwin' yo'self at him?'

Topaze raved.

'He loved me, Ah tell yo'.' A chorus of mocking contempt was flung at Topaze. Another chorus girl flung back at her:

'Yeah, an' same time he told Carrie, who was singer at duh Web, dat he was crazy fo' her.' Another chimed in:

'An' wasn't he roun' Nigger Mike's spendin' ever't'ing that yo' all handed over to him?'

'Didn't Harry Wray dancin' wit' me only a few nights ago say Money Johnson come aroun' an' gambled duh money yo' give him, at Doggie's pool room? What yo' yelpin' like dat fo', Topaze?'

'It's a damn lie!' Topaze shrieked, infuriated by the taunts of the others.

''Tain't neither. Ah'll prove it by Harry. Money Johnson boasted he could git all duh money he wanted fum yo'.'

'You're jealous sluts. All o' yo'.' Topaze was crying with rage. She turned to Gert. 'Gert, yo' know right here in this joint Money Johnson kissed me an' tol' me he loved me better'n anythin' in duh world. Ain't dat right, Gert?'

'Ah don't remember, but he mought.'

'Yo' was settin' him up in yo' apartment, feedin him

chicken and buyin' his clo'es. Di'n't cost him nothin' to say he love yo'.'

'Gert, yo' don' know nothin'. He proposed to me. We was goin' to be married. We was goin' to Paris when Bert was takin' me over wit' his show.'

'Yo' was goin' to take him, yo' mean. Why di'n't he take yo' when he made his money in the number racket? Went over by hisself, di'n't he, an' turned yo' over cold?'

'He was goin' to send fo' me.'

'Went over wit' another gal an' made yo' grieve till yo' went on duh dope an' lost yo' job. Ruined yo'self fo' him, dat's whut yo' did.'

'Don't care what yo' all say. He loved me.'

'Well, den he di'n't want no mo' ob yo' after he got big an' prosp'rous an' grand, an' got hisself a white woman 'stead o' yo',' observed Gert as she passed around the liquor.

Topaze threw her head in the air and exulted.

'Yeah, an' Ah fixed her. She won't be actin' up grand no mo' now he's in a gaol house.' She broke into a spasm of uncontrollable hysterical laughter.

'Stop dat sinful mule laugh.' Gert was shaking her. 'Neighbours'll complain to duh owner o' dese premises. Den where duh hell Ah goin' to be fo' a livin'?'

Topaze screamed with frenzied glee.

'Hush up, will yo'? Hush up before Ah smack yo'.'

'Damn silly way to get back yo' man, puttin' duh bulls on him fo' runnin' a policy game. Jus' spitin' yo'self over a slut white woman!'

'She's duh no account trash yo' should 'a took it out on.'

Topaze gave herself over to depressive abandon. She flung open the window and was half out when she was dragged back. Gert was in a terror of alarm.

What yo' mean by disgracin' mah place with yo' goddam suicidin'? Think of mah reputation and do your carrin's on somewhere else.'

The bell rang.

'Mah gawd! Who's dat? Now whut yo' goin' to do?' Gert asked Topaze who was still struggling in the window. 'Fall out er stay in, while Ah sees who's at duh do'. Make up yo' mind!'

The girls finally dragged Topaze to the sofa.

'Ah'm sorry Ah put him in gaol,' she sobbed. 'But he done said he loved me.'

'Ah, nuts. Dat's whut he told ever' one o' us here. But we ain't goin' to hell over it, like yo's aiming to.'

Cokey Jenny walked in with Gert.

'Hello, everybody,' Jenny greeted them. 'Just come up for a shot of liquor. Feelin' low. Things is rotten. What's the matter with Topaze?'

'Just goin' out duh window to put a knife in dat Gordon scum yo' used to hang aroun' wit',' one said.

Jenny removed her hat.

'I ain't seen her since Money grabbed her off,' she said. 'Guess she's laying low till the ball an' chain's off his leg.'

'Lak hell she is!' Topaze was on her feet, and shouting again.

Jenny stared and said.

'Lou and Harry told me they don't know nothin' about her, ain't seen her in weeks.'

Topaze laughed fiendishly.

'Well, Ah know where she is. In her place where duh bastard ought to be! Where she won't get no mo' uplift fum Money Johnson!'

'Yeah? Where is she?' Jenny's attention was riveted on Topaze.

'In duh Baldwin Five an' Ten store.'

'Since when?'

'All duh time she been wit' Money Johnson. She's sellin' stuff over duh counter. Hundreds o' dollars' worth ever' day.'

'Who says?'

'Ah knows a white woman who gits it fum her. Here's how she gits it.' Topaze thrust her hand into her bosom and brought out a gold-plated rouge compact.

Jenny's cold eyes became dark pools of hate and her cruel lips drew taut. A sinister leer gashed her face, which suddenly appeared like a death mask. Only the eyes gave evidence of life.

'Ah knows plenty about her activities,' Topaze said. 'An' believe me she won't bother Money Johnson no mo', what with me knowin' about this.' She held up the compact like a torch of freedom.

Jenny looked like a blanched carcass as she sat silently drinking her gin. Finished, she drew up her skirt, pulled out a greasy dollar bill from her stocking, paid Gert and started for the door.

'Goin'?'

Jenny nodded her head in a daze, and with eyes looking grimly into space shuffled out into the hall. Once in the street she walked and walked, unaware of direction, indifferent to traffic.

So! That was why she hadn't seen Babe. Pretty cute! No one thought of looking for her in a Five and Ten Cent store. Diamonds and ermine, and a car that was a jewel case, and a rich nigger keeping her.

'The double-crossin' heel!' ripped across Jenny's mind. 'Came up to Harlem, gits my confidence, and then makes Lou and Harry give her the job that would've put me on easy street. The lowdown dog. The dirty two-face! She'd rob the gold tooth out of her mother's head an' cut her sister's throat for a buck! She never came around to give a pal a good time when she got a break. All for herself any way you looked at it. The garbage-can maggot! Lower than dirt! Just no good! Stole the job I would've got if I hadn't put her wise to it. The cesspool eel! To do that to a pal! Peddlin' the 'junk' in the Five and Ten. Hundreds of dollars' worth a day. Fat percentage! I'm bein' done out of a fortune. No wonder Lou and Harry closed up on me. Said the proposition fell through. Said that was the racket they meant to cut me in on. I'd of cleaned up. Now, what've I got? Lou an' Harry pulls me out of the Pavillion, tellin' me they don't want to pay no more police graft for that spot! Well, pretty Babe Gordon, this is the last time you pull a dirty deal on me. An' the last time Lou an' Harry gives me the double-X. Goddam 'em!'

The next day Jenny appeared in the Baldwin Five and Ten Cent store. Mingling with the crowd, she drifted from one counter to another until she saw Babe, who certainly didn't look like the same broad that had been sparkling round with Money Johnson. But she couldn't see anything phony. The counter where Babe worked was loaded with cosmetics of all kinds, in all manner of cases. Jenny couldn't tell who was buying dope that way.

Then suddenly she recognized the lily-white girl with the wan face and the delicate long fingers to whom she had sold dope in Toni's joint. The girl made a purchase of Babe. Jenny watched her go out and a uniformed chauffeur follow. Jenny waited ten minutes longer on the look-out for familiar faces. Then she strolled up to Babe's counter.

Babe greeted Jenny as if she had been eagerly expecting her call every day. Jenny felt at a disadvantage, but knew Babe wouldn't be able to talk herself out of the drop she had on her now.

'Hello, Jenny,' said Babe. 'Ain't it tough what happened to me, an' I got to work like this to make a livin'?'

'Yeah,' said Jenny. 'You been havin' such a hard time in Harlem, ain't you?'

'Bearcat and me split up.'

'Yeah, an' you got a baby to support and the insurance to keep up. Ain't it hell?'

'Honest, Jenny, I got so much to tell you. I was comin' up all week to see you. How's things?'

'Bad enough so I got to be lookin' over things in a Five and Ten.'

'Ain't it a scream, me bein' here?'

Jenny bared her teeth in a ghastly grin.

'Yes, it sure handed me a wallop, meeting you this way.'

'Y'never know what life's goin' to hand you, Jenny.'

'Yer right. It's sure tough you had to come down to this – punchin' dimes for Baldwin. Bet you're broken-hearted you had to give up Bearcat and Money Johnson for this.'

'Oh,' said Babe, feeling sure she was convincing Jenny that she was on the level. 'I got to stay here if I expect to get alimony from the Bearcat.'

Jenny appeared surprised.

'Is that what you aim to get by bein' here?'

'Sure! He can't get nothing on me so long as I work hard to support myself.'

'Look out you don't take up religion next!'

'Just the same, Jen, say a prayer for me.'

'Yeah, you might need savin',' Jenny smiled. 'So long, Babe.'

'Droppin' in again?'

'I might.'

Jenny faded away in the crowd. Babe didn't like the way Jenny had smiled.

It was several days before Babe saw Jenny again. And then in strange circumstances.

• • • • • •

'Cash! . . . Cash! . . . Cash!'

'Mr. Valentine – oh, Mr. Valentine! Five dollars' worth of dimes, please!'

It was the peak of the day's business at Baldwin's. The neighbourhood populace was streaming in and out of the four entrances of the store. Forward at the left wall, the player piano was reeling off, 'What a Friend I have in Jesus.'

Opposite against the right wall at the phonograph record counter, the electric orthophonic played, 'Save It, Pretty Mama, All for Me, Don't Give Any of It Away.'

Between the records and the store front, at the white tiled lunch counter, a little old white-haired lady in black was having tea and nabiscos. A plumber in greasy overalls bolted down spaghetti. Three negro girls discussed Lon Chaney's latest picture over ice cream and coconut cake, and a fat woman poured down buttermilk. On a line with the lunch counter to the rear of the store was the jewellery counter flashing with necklaces of pearl, coral, amber and glass; trays of rings, ear-drops, brooches, where fair Africa bejewelled herself.

Between the second and third entrances of the store, near the candy bazaar, was the frankfurter stand, where a negro minister munched a hot dog, while he consoled a thin young negro woman with black crape trailing from the back of her hat.

Starting the fourth row of bazaars was the women's hosiery counter where a beehive of women, black and white, buzzed over the leg art. Next in line came the cosmetic counter where the toilet lotions shimmered in gorgeous many-coloured bottles, presided over by the no less colourful Babe Gordon.

A group of chorus girls with blue-black hair and soft brown eyes trooped up to Babe's counter and greeted her enthusiastically. Caroline led the peppery chatter.

'Hello, Babe, here's yo' black tulips from the Net. How is yo', honey?'

'Fine, Caroline,' said Babe. 'How are you girls?'

'Jus' grand, honey,' Emma, a slender, bronze-skinned girl replied. 'What's duh matter, angel, yo' don't drop roun' to duh club oftener?'

'A hard-workin' girl like me has got to get some sleep nights.'

A little black dwarfed girl, who was the comedienne of the revue they were working in, laughed with a deep bray, rolled her eyes, and said,

'Stop yo' shuckin', Miss Gordon. Bet yo' got mo' real estate in yo' name dan Ah got kinks in mah coiffure.'

The girls exploded with laughter.

'Listen to dat gal crack!'

'Ain't she somethin' scandalous wit' her 'whiffs'.'

The dwarf's white teeth shone like polished ivory. She dug among the lipsticks. 'Miss Babe, ain't yo' got mah carmine?'

Emma laughed.

'Carmine? Listen, Helen, yo' ugly enough wit'out makin' yo'self Spanish.'

'Ah ain't fixin' to look Spanish. It's a sinful effect Ah's after.'

The girls shrieked at that.

'Yo' homely as sin wit'out dat.'

Babe handed the girl a lipstick.

'There's your carmine, Helen.'

Esther, who was one of the gang, asked for cold cream with bleach in it.

'What yo' care about bleach, Esther, when yo' got eyes like dat?'

The dwarf was cuttin' up hilarious again. 'It's duh eyes what contain duh magic o' love. Just give me a pair o' eyes what Ah can presdigidate wit' an' Ah make any man think I got all duh rest.'

'Golly!' Emma cried. 'He got to, wit' dem wishbone legs yo' got.'

Another girl came in to tell them to shake it up for rehearsal. The girls picked up their purchases.

'Ain't got a friend wants to buy a second-han' racehorse, has yo', Miss Babe?' Helen asked.

Emma laughed.

'Yo' draggin' in dat nag again, Helen?'

'Ah took him 'stead o' cash when Ah hit duh numbers. He got a excel'n' pedigree — '

'Only needs four new legs. Come on, Venus.'

'Say,' said Caroline, leaning over the counter close to Babe. 'Too bad about Money Johnson, ain't it, honey? He be out soon though.'

'So long, Miss Gordon,' said Helen.

'Bye-bye, Miss Babe,' said Emma.

'Come on down soon,' said Esther.

The black tulips went out of the door.

'Cash! . . . Cash! . . . Cash!'

'Five dollars' worth of dimes, Mr. Thomas, please,' called Babe.

Mr. Thomas, the floor manager, a serious, pleasant-looking man with the smothered eyes of a resigned drudge, received two packages of dimes from the cashier and brought them to the perfume counter and handed them to Babe, who gave him a rumpled five-dollar bill in exchange. A dance hall girl with a skirt vainly tying to reach her knees rushed up to the root beer counter and called for a mug of brew. A sleepy, shuffling black mama wheeling a baby carriage sauntered in with a piece of salmon cloth between her fingers, to be matched.

A white woman with a pallid face, twitching mouth, and fluttering fingers stopped at Babe's counter, idled over the cosmetics, picked up an ounce vial of perfume, palmed it to Babe with a bill and a dime. Babe looked at the bill, wrapped the glass bottle and a compact case and handed it to the customer. She rang up the dime on the register.

Babe was first aware that Jenny was in the store when she spotted her three counters away. A man in a brown suit and another one with a black derby hat were close behind her.

Babe began to have nervous tremors. If only she had seen them before. She had just sold some stuff to the frail-looking girl with the slender embalmed fingers, who, clasping the package against her breast, was still idling about the aisles. Why the hell didn't she get out! The chauffeur was waiting for her by the door.

Babe felt sure now that those purposeful-looking men with Jenny were detectives.

Jenny was moving towards the pale girl with the incriminating package.

There were four cartons of dope-loaded compacts under Babe's counter. How to get rid of them? It sure looked like Jenny had squealed.

Just then Rose, the girl who helped get Babe her job, and who worked at he adjoining counter where manicuring articles were on display, stepped over and asked.

'Say, Babe, have we got any more orange sticks around here, or will I have to send down to the stockroom? There's a lady here who wants an orange stick!'

Babe felt her heart leap.

'Look under my counter, Rose,' she said.

When Rose bent down to look under the counter Babe stooped down with her. She seized the four cartons and thrust them into Rose's hands.

'For God's sake, Rose, take these down to the stockroom and hide them good. Make believe you're looking for something down there. I'll watch your counter for you.'

'All right,' said Rose.

'Hurry!' said Babe.

Rose headed for the back of the store and hurried down the employees' stairs to the stockroom.

Babe, with a gasp of relief, turned to the impatient customer at Rose's counter.

'Sorry, lady,' she said. 'But we ain't got any more orange sticks up here. I just sent down to the storeroom. If you will wait a few minutes they'll be up.'

'No,' said the customer. 'I'll step in to-morrow.'

Thank God! thought Babe. She turned and saw the two men with Jenny suddenly seize the girl who had bought a compact from her just a little while ago. If the girl squawked, she was done for.

One man snatched the girl's package from her. The other held her arms securely above the elbows. She clawed desperately for the parcel which the detective was opening. Becoming hysterical she let out a piercing scream, then fainted dead away.

Mr. Thomas, the store manager, elbowed his way through the crowd, shouting that everything was all right, and for the clerks not to leave their posts.

The detectives of the narcotic squad showed the manager their credentials as they stooped over to pick up the stricken girl.

Roughly grabbing the limp form, they carried her into the manager's office at the back of the store.

'I beg of you gentlemen,' the manager said excitedly to the officers, 'not to take any action until I have informed Mr. Baldwin about what has taken place.'

One of the detectives held up the compact he had found in the store package.

'There's four two-and-a-half-grain cubes of morphine in there. Ask Mr. Baldwin to explain that.'

Wayne Baldwin, sitting in his private office at the Fifth Avenue headquarters of the Baldwin Stores, Inc., received the startling report from the Harlem branch. Giving the local manager every assurance of immediate co-operation, he first notified the company's attorney, then hurried from his office, jumped into a taxi, and made for Harlem.

While the manager was telephoning the big boss, one of the detectives checked over the contents of the girl's package. There were, besides the dope filled compact, a ten cent bottle of perfume and a cash register receipt from counter nineteen. That was Babe's counter.

Holding the receipt as an important piece of evidence, the officer turned to the manager and in a solemn voice said, 'Send for the girl in charge of counter nineteen!'

19

BABE'S LUCK

O'BRIEN, chief of the legal staff of the Baldwin Stores, Inc., took the subway and arrived at the Harlem branch store long before Wayne Baldwin, whose taxi meanwhile was picking its way through the barriers of heavy traffic.

He found the detectives grilling the society girl, who, having been restored to consciousness, proved to be a stubborn case, though obviously weak and nervous.

They were trying to force a confession from her with sharp, pointed questions.

'Where did you get this compact?'

'Who sold it to you?'

'You got it in this store, didn't you?'

'How much did you pay for it?'

'You had a chauffeur with you. One of our men is holding him outside. You don't look like the kind of a girl that goes to a Five and Ten to shop. It'll be better for you to tell the truth. Come clean now. Who did you get this from?'

To all these questions, the girl either answered, 'No,' or shook her head, refusing to say anything.

'See here, officer,' said Mr. Thomas, the manager, 'your line of questions is leading up to some very serious conclusions, which may compromise a concern doing a business of millions.'

'We can't help that,' snapped the man in the derby. 'We got this girl with the goods and we're goin' to find out how she got the dope, where she got it, and who she got it from. All we can prove right now is that she's guilty of havin' morphine on her. If we find she got it from one of the clerks in your store, you go to the station house with us along with whoever sold her the stuff.'

'You'll see that the store is not implicated,' said Thomas, 'when the salesgirl from counter nineteen comes in. We only employ girls who are well recommended.'

'That don't mean a thing. Anybody can fake references,' said the detective in the baggy brown suit. Then the door to the office opened and Babe Gordon was ushered in.

Outside the store, things were going on the same as ever. In fact, the majority of the sales force and customers were unaware that anything unusual had occurred. A few had seen a girl faint and be carried into the rear of the store, where for all they knew she had been revived and permitted to go home. A number of detectives who were detailed to search the store were working around unobtrusively; they might have been employees of the Baldwin organization checking up on store activities.

The officer who had escorted Babe to the manager's office now reported to the detective in the derby, who was evidently in command.

'We're still lookin' around, Chief, but we ain't turned up anythin' yet.'

The firm's lawyer ran his eye over Babe and decided he had better question this girl before the detectives tried any rough stuff.

Mr. Thomas introduced Babe to those in the room with the remark, 'This is Miss Gordon, in charge of counter nineteen. She's one of the best salesgirls we've got.'

'Miss Gordon,' O'Brien said, 'I want to ask you a few questions. There's no need of your being frightened unless you really have cause to be. However, I believe you haven't. Just tell us the truth. That's all we ask.'

The truth! All Babe knew was that she'd have to get out of the jam. The hell with anything else!

She opened her eyes wide and veiled them with a look of innocence, of not knowing what all the excitement was about.

'What do you want to ask me? If I saw that girl faint?'

A detective started to speak, but O'Brien beat him to it.

'No, Miss Gordon,' he said. 'We have a record that you made a sale to this young lady. What did you sell her?'

'A ten cent bottle of perfume. Ain't it on the slip?'

'Yes. But are you sure you sold her nothing else?'

Babe frowned.

'What are you doin'? Tryin' to accuse me of gyppin'?'

'Not at all. We have here a rouge compact that we thought she might have obtained in this store.'

'Well, she didn't get it from my counter.'

One of the detectives leaned forward.

'Do you know what's in that compact?'

'Sure,' said Babe. 'Rouge!'

The detective looked disappointed at her reply. O'Brien smiled covertly. She was a quick one, he thought.

The detective turned to O'Brien.

'We got a tip-off that this here Miss Babe Gordon was peddlin' dope in this store.'

'Well, where is the person who accuses this girl?' O'Brien inquired. 'That's a pretty serious charge and you should have something to back it up.'

'I've got men out there makin' a thorough search,' the detective said. 'And we haven't looked in this girl's pocket-book yet.'

Babe offered to produce her pocket-book from her locker. The detective accompanied her to the locker room, she took out her purse, and both returned to the office.

'There it is,' said Babe, handing him the purse. 'Look all you want.'

So it was Jenny who had squealed!

The detective in the derby took the bag and went through it carefully, even feeling the lining. He examined a roll of bills. There was fifty dollars in it.

'Lot of money,' he said, 'for a girl workin' in a store like this to have at one time.'

'I been savin' that up for weeks to get a new dress.'

The office door opened and a plain-clothes man came in.

'Nothin' doin' outside, Chief,' he said.

The detective grunted, and pointed at the society girl. 'Take her to headquarters. Maybe she'll talk there, when she finds out the stretch she's facin'.'

'I've told you all I'm going to tell you,' said the girl listlessly – 'which is nothing.'

She was resolved that they never would get a word out of her. Her family would have to know of her arrest, but they were influential and would employ every means possible to shield and protect her. Besides, she knew that her system, long inured to drugs, would start its old craving again, and then she would have to depend on Babe and her associates. She didn't dare inform the police.

'Couldn't get nothin' out of her chauffeur either,' said the plain-clothes.

'Well, take her along,' said the chief of detectives. 'There's something damn funny about this whole thing.'

'I'm afraid you've been misled, my friend,' said O'Brien with a smile. 'Call me up if there's any further development that might be of interest to us.'

As the detectives and the girl passed out, the chief turned to Babe.

'We'll have an eye on you from now on, young lady.'

'Well, look out you don't get somethin' in it,' said Babe, with a mocking laugh. She knew she was safe now.

O'Brien walked across to a door leading into an adjoining private office and opened it.

'Will you wait in here for a little while, Miss Gordon?' As she passed through the doorway he stopped her. 'Oh, by the way, the detective said something about being tipped off that you were selling drugs in this store. Do you know of anyone who might have a grudge against you and want to do you harm?'

Babe looked at him for a moment in silence.

'Yes,' she said. 'I think I know who started this mess.'

'You do?'

'Yeah. It was a dame who's jealous of me. She's a bad one. Tried to knife me once. And she's liable to make more trouble if she gets the chance.'

'Well, now,' said O'Brien with a friendly smile. 'We're not going to give her the chance, if we can prevent it. What makes you suspect this girl?'

'I saw her come into the store with those detectives.'

O'Brien rubbed the side of his face meditatively.

'This girl . . . Do you think we might be able to do something to – er – keep her quiet?'

Babe nodded.

'She'll do anything for money.'

'All right. I'll see what I can do. Will you be good enough to give me her name and address?'

Babe complied, giving the attorney an address where she felt certain Cokey Jenny could be reached.

'Thanks,' said O'Brien. 'Now please wait a few minutes.' He closed the door after her.

Mr. Thomas, who had seen to it that the detectives removed the society girl by a side entrance so as not to cause a disturbance in the store, now returned to the office with Wayne Baldwin, who had just arrived on the scene. Baldwin came in with an anxious look, but his attorney quickly allayed his fears. O'Brien told him everything that had taken place, and when he suggested that they do something to keep Cokey Jenny from making more trouble, Baldwin agreed.

'Of course,' said the attorney, 'you will have to let this girl – Miss Gordon – go, for the detectives have threatened to watch her. It will be better for her and for the store. As for the girl who was arrested, my theory is that she had the compact when she came in the store. Although I can't see for the life of me why a girl like that, who is obviously wealthy, should come in here to buy perfume, and then have her rouge stick in one of our paper bags.'

'Perhaps she likes our perfume,' said Baldwin with a grin.

O'Brien laughed.

'Well, whatever her motive, I think we needn't worry about the store being involved. I'll take care of everything and make a report to you later.'

'All right,' said Baldwin, 'you can run along. I want to see that things are straightened out here. Besides, I'd like to talk to this girl, this Miss Gordon. From what you've said about the way she conducted herself during the investigation, she must be pretty clever. Its rather tough on her, firing her this way. But I suppose I'll have to. Where is she now?'

'In the next office,' said O'Brien. 'Well, I'll see you to-morrow.'

Baldwin turned to the manager, when O'Brien had gone.

'You had better get a new girl for that counter right away.'

'Miss Gordon was a very good salesgirl, Mr. Baldwin,' said the manager.

'Well, it is too bad,' said Baldwin, 'but it can't be helped.'

The manager went out. Baldwin rose and crossed to the other office. He opened the door slightly and said:

'Come in, Miss.' Then he seated himself behind the manager's desk. He didn't like the job of discharging people. He regretted that he hadn't left it to the manager. But he wanted the girl to leave without feeling that she had been treated unfairly.

He heard the office door close and looked up.

'Sit down, Miss — ' he began and broke off. His mouth almost fell open in amazement. His eyes closed for an instant and then opened and stared. 'Good God!' he thought. 'Am I dreaming? Is this, can this be, the girl I saw at the Harlem Breakfast Club, wearing ermine and diamonds? Yes, I couldn't forget her face. I stared at it too long that night ever to forget it! What in heaven's name is she doing here?'

All his emotions that had been so stirred on first seeing Babe broke into flame again. He couldn't find the words he wanted to say.

His one thought was that he must never let her go. He must hold her at all costs.

As for Babe, she too was experiencing a swift stirring of emotions. Her eyes fastened themselves on Baldwin's face and her heart just seemed to turn over. All she could murmur to herself was: 'Oh, God! Ain't he swell! Oh, I could die lookin' at him!' Here was a man she wanted more than she had ever wanted anything in her life before.

'Er – sit down, Miss Gordon,' Baldwin managed to repeat. His eyes feasted themselves hungrily on her. Did she suspect anything, he wondered – the conflict within himself, the turmoil her presence caused him? But no, that was impossible!

He cleared his throat and made an heroic effort to speak.

'Miss Gordon,' he began, 'er – this has been – er – very unfortunate, this affair. It has been – er – embarrassing for all of us. Mr. Thomas tells me you've done very well here. I – er – we – er – would not want you to suffer for something for which you were in no way to blame.'

She sat in a chair near the desk clinging to every word. 'Oh,' she thought, 'he's the most marvellous thing that ever lived?'

'It would be useless for you to stay here,' Baldwin continued, 'for you no doubt have a very bitter enemy in this – er – girl Mr. O'Brien was telling me about. She might do you harm and injure the store's reputation. Now, I've had an idea for some time concerning a new advertising campaign on certain products we feature in our stores. I am sure you would be useful in our promotion department. It would mean a better position with plenty of opportunity to advance. I – er – should be glad to see to that personally. By the way, this new position would require some posing for pictures to be used in our advertising. Have you ever done any posing?'

'Oh yes,' said Babe. 'I used to be a model for suits and dresses.'

'Splendid! This will be easy for you. I might have you posed with – er – say, those new Sun-Glo hair-nets, for blonde hair, you know. Er – I'll take it up with our advertising manager at once. Er – I'd like to discuss this with you more fully, before you take up the actual work. Er – have you an engagement for this evening, Miss Gordon?'

'I certainly wouldn't turn down a date with a swell feller like this,' Babe told herself. 'Gee, I'd better watch my language with him. He's the original high-hat.'

These thoughts flashed through her mind in a second.

'I haven't planned anything for this evening,' she replied, after carefully choosing her words.

'Well, then,' he said, 'suppose we talk things over at dinner somewhere. Perhaps, later, we can go to the theatre together. You know, I really owe you something for the splendid way you behaved under cross examination by those stupid detectives. It must have been very unpleasant. Now, I could stop for you in my car, if you'll give me your address. Or, if you prefer, I can meet you elsewhere. What do you say?'

'I'd love it,' said Babe, and she meant it. She had returned to her apartment in Washington Heights when Money went to gaol, so she gave him her address.

'I'll be there, then,' he said, 'at seven sharp.'

She arose to go, and extended her hand to him. 'Thank you so much,' she said.

As Baldwin clasped her soft hand, he experienced a new surge of emotion. So she had been here all the time! The woman he had searched for all these weeks had been right here in his own employ. Feeling rather tremulous with joy, he opened the office door for Babe and nodded a formal dismissal.

20

HIGH-HAT

BABE prepared for her evening engagement with Wayne Baldwin with more care than she had ever expended on herself. She wanted to attract him, because he not only appealed to her senses but he also represented that world of society she had enviously followed through the newspapers, and occasionally viewed in the erotic atmosphere of Harlem.

Babe had learned the rudiments of refinement from her association with more or less cultured people who, as fight fans, were interested in the Bearcat when he showed promise of being a champion. She also had observed the manners of the socially elect in the various joy places of Harlem. She knew how to put on the Ritz, and realized she must appear well bred in order to create a good impression on Baldwin. She did not know, of course, that she had made an impression on him long before – an impression that was a deep and lasting one.

'What shall I wear? Something conservative to create a modest impression? Or something gay? No, I'll wear my white satin and ermine wrap. That's most alluring, and I want to lure him. Gee ! But he's swell. What about my diamonds? Yes, I'll wear them too. What will he say about the diamonds? But no, he won't ask. He'll just think, and that's what I want him to do – think!'

So she wore the ermine wrap and the same gown she had worn the morning Baldwin had seen her at the Harlem Breakfast Club. She glittered with the brilliant diamonds Money Johnson had given her, and she hoped Baldwin would like her appearance. She didn't know his memory would be tortured by the vision she presented.

At seven o'clock, Baldwin's new Cadillac sixteen glided up to the kerb. She was ready long before he rang the bell of her apartment. When she opened the door he stood breathless before her beauty, but, quickly regaining his customary ease of manner, he said smilingly:

'Well, this is a pleasant surprise. From past experiences I though one always had to wait for a woman. And the more charming the woman, the longer one had to wait. But I'm glad to find that the most charming woman I have ever met is ready on time.'

Babe decided then and there never to be so prompt again, but it was the first time she had ever stepped out with a real swell.

When they reached the motor, the chauffeur opened the tonneau door for them. There wasn't the gaudy flash to this car that characterized Money Johnson's. This car was like the man beside her – distinguished, reserved, mannered.

They were driven to a quiet restaurant, where the food was excellent. A stringed orchestra played softly, weaving a tapestry of sound as a background for their conversation.

Baldwin said nothing to Babe about having seen her before to-day. As he watched her, the thought of the negro continued to haunt him, but he decided never to mention the episode to her.

Babe expected to hear something about her new job, but he said nothing about it. His conversation was more personal, more subtly flattering to her. He commented on her taste in clothes, hinting that it must be difficult to manage such a smart appearance on a small income. Then he talked about himself.

Babe reasoned: 'I guess he likes my type. That's why he invited me out. He didn't want to talk about the job.' She felt that before the evening was over he was going to 'proposition' her. He was the kind of a guy that could get any woman he wanted.

With a fluttering heart and watchful eyes, Babe carried on a rather halting conversation during the delightful dinner Wayne had ordered. Then they hurried off to the theatre and saw one of the season's most popular musical reviews. It was after the theatre on the way back to her apartment in Wayne's car that he really lost control of himself. Seizing Babe in his arms, he suddenly changed from the polished society man to a primitive male hungry and thirsty for her body.

This new Baldwin Babe understood perfectly as she gave herself to his kisses. She was shrewd enough not to allow him to enter her apartment when they finally reached Washington Heights. There would have to be many dinners and many long tantalizing evenings before she would give herself completely to him.

But Wayne's powers of persuasion, which were one with her own desires, proved too much for a will that had never practised restraint.

Within a fortnight she had moved again, accepting from Baldwin a beautifully furnished Riverside Drive apartment, a Rolls Royce, and Pearl, a negro maid. Here she took her place among the hundreds of other mistresses who gaze with languorous, well-paid eyes across the moon-silvered Hudson.

Her wardrobe was filled with exquisite dresses and gowns. She had her own bank account, as Baldwin deposited a fat cheque to her credit once a month. Besides that he took her wherever she wanted to go without caring in the least whether he was seen by members of his own set.

The nights he spend with Babe in her apartment – their apartment, as he thought of it – were hours of pure unalloyed happiness passing all too quickly.

The shadow of the black man who had loved her was gradually fading out of Babe's mind. Baldwin entirely forgot the past, he was so intoxicated by the present. And as for the future – well, that could take care of itself.

Babe had cast off all the old roughness of her past. She appeared the well-kept lady. No courtesan of the sixteenth century was more beautiful than this one of the twentieth, none more successful in holding a much-desired lover.

Little wonder, then, that this was the high moment of Babe's life. She was nineteen now, and the years when she would have to worry about crow's-feet and wrinkles were far away.

But the ways of the gods are strange and they give happiness sparingly to humanity. Perhaps they thought Babe's was unearned happiness. At any rate, they began to weave shadows for her.

Pearl, Babe's maid, on her nights off was a frequenter of Nigger Gert's. Pearl, it seemed, loved 'corn' and gin. It was there in Gert's that she raved about the beauty and generosity of her mistress. Cokey Jenny sat and listened, for she, too, often dropped into Gert's for a drink.

'Goddam the luck!' Jenny thought. 'Here they give me two hundred bucks to keep my mouth shut about Babe sellin' dope, and she ups and grabs off the guy who owns the whole works. A millionaire that makes Money Johnson look like a pedlar. Well, if that slut ain't got a rabbit's foot.'

She questioned the maid and got Babe's address and telephone number out of her. Well, Babe would have to come across this time – come across plenty, or . . . A murderous light burned in Jenny's dope-glazed eyes.

Jenny began her dirty work by calling up Babe's apartment and trying to get her on the telephone. Babe answered it once, and when she recognized Jenny's voice she pretended she was the maid and said that Miss Gordon was not at home. After that, she instructed Pearl to say that she was out whenever Jenny called up.

She wondered how Jenny had obtained her phone number, which was not listed in the directory. One evening, when Pearl was doing her hair, she found out.

'Dis girl dat's callin' yo' up,' said Pearl, 'say she yo' friend. But Ah don' believe she no friend o' yours. She don' look like duh kind yo'd have any truck wit', ma'am.'

Babe looked at Pearl in surprise.

'How do you know what she looks like, Pearl? Have you seen her?'

'Yes, ma'am. Ah done meet her up at Nigger Gert's, dat's a place Ah goes sometimes. She was dere when Ah was tellin' some o' duh girls how kind yo' is to me, an' she say, she an old friend o' yours an' dat she just dyin' to see yo'. So Ah gives her yo' telephone number.'

'You did?'

'Yes, ma'am. Ah hope Ah ain't done wrong. She say she know yo'd be glad to heah fum her. She say she got some-thin' important to talk to yo' about. So Ah asks her where yo' could get a-hold o' her. She says she ain't got no way yo' could get in touch wit' her, she'd have to call yo' up. So not knowin' whut it was about Ah done give her yo' number.'

Babe thought a minute.

'Well, the next time she calls up, Pearl, let me talk to her. I've got to stop her calling up here. She's bad, Pearl, and I don't want to have anything to do with her.'

'Yes, ma'am. She kind of dopy lookin' like she hit duh pipe or somepin.'

Babe smiled. She surmised that Jenny was travelling the trail of dreams faster than ever, now that the breaks were against her.

She told Baldwin that Jenny was annoying her, and explained that she felt the girl was trying to shake her down.

'You're right,' Baldwin told her. 'She's just trying to black-mail you. But don't pay any attention to her. She can't do you any harm.'

Babe was not so sure, but as Jenny did not call up for several days she began to think that perhaps Jenny had given up trying to see her, or perhaps was too doped to remember the past.

Babe was too happy to worry much about anything. Her apartment was so charming that she hated to go out alone during the day. The windows of her living-room and bedroom looked out across the Drive to the Hudson, with its river life that appealed to her imagination. Some day, she thought, I will go with Wayne on a boat. A big boat sailing for Europe. It was all rather vague in her mind, for her longest voyage had been on a ferry boat to Jersey.

She had had her bedroom decorated according to her own taste. The two large windows were hung with violet plush portières that could be drawn open or shut by heavy gold tasselled cords. At night the room could be made a blaze of light by a glass electrolier suspended from the ceiling with ropes of shimmering crystals.

Huge French plate mirrors studded the pale green-tinted walls. A dressing-table completely designed in mirror pieces stood between the two windows. Lying in bed she could see herself in it, and every move she made. She had derived her taste for all this glass that reflected her movements from Money Johnson.

A four-poster bed of gold and jade-green with its violet and gold counterpane dominated the room.

Baldwin satisfied her every desire, and Babe loved him more and more as the days slipped quickly by. She knew she could hold him, or any man for that matter, so she saw her future as just a succession of nights of pleasure blend-ing into . . . For the first time in her life Babe became maternal.

Then Jenny again! Just when she was beginning to forget about her. Just when life seemed so secure.

Pearl brought her the message that Jenny was on the wire. With a flash of anger, Babe sprang up and went to the phone. Yet something warned her to handle Jenny with kid gloves.

'Hello,' she said coldly.

'This you, Babe?' Jenny inquired.

'Yes,' said Babe. 'My maid tells me you've been calling up here quite often. What's on your mind? What do you want?'

'Yeah, your maid,' said Jenny. 'Pretty lucky jane, ain'tcha? Got a swell apartment, a maid an' everything. It's a wonder you wouldn't invite a feller up.'

'Well, I've been very busy,' said Babe.

'Too busy to see an old friend, eh?' Jenny said.

'I'm not seeing anybody,' Babe replied.

'Well, I gotta see you,' said Jenny. 'I got somethin' to say to you, you'd be interested in.'

'I know what you want, Jenny,' said Babe. 'But you can't get anything out of me.'

'No?' Jenny drawled. 'Well, listen to me, kid. You better be nice to your old friend Jenny. 'Cause — '

Babe's voice echoed her anger.

'Don't try to scare me, Jenny. I know you played a dirty trick on me. You've done enough, and from now on we're quits. If you keep bothering me, I'll have you sent up the river. Don't forget I can talk to the police too, if I want to. And I've got more protection than you have.'

Jenny's voice was menacing.

'Oh, so that's the way you feel about it? Turnin' down an old pal.'

'That old pal stuff makes me sick,' said Babe. 'Don't bother calling up here again.'

'All right,' said Jenny. 'But don't forget I got me finger on ya. You can't get away wit' that stuff on me.'

Babe jammed down the receiver.

Jenny flew out of the telephone booth in a rage. She was literally shaking with anger.

'I'll spoil her racket,' she murmured. She was all in a lather. Perspiration stood out in cold beads on her forehead. She went into a convenient hallway and had a sniff.

Her mind made viciously clear, for the time being, by the drug she had taken, Jenny began to formulate a plan of revenge upon Babe, who was the object of all Jenny's concentrated hate.

She would tell the story of Babe's life to ears that would be deeply interested. She would tell Baldwin. Show him what a tart he had set up as a queen. But no – that wouldn't do. He was too gone on Babe to believe her. There would be no use in going to him. After Babe once got a man physically he'd forget everything and forgive everything.

Jenny had a new thought. Her pallid lips twisted in a horrible grin. She'd show her! She'd go to his folks and spill the dirt so they'd make Baldwin kick Babe out. Jenny sought a telephone directory. She found the W. W. Baldwin Stores, Inc., and its list of local branches. Then under that, Baldwin, W. W., residence, and number. She made note of the street address, closed the book and started off. Now, she thought, she'd knock Babe's luck for a loop.

Jenny found her way to the Baldwin residence, and pressed the bell. She looked, in her shabby clothes and cheap hat with a drab feather, like a wet, half-strangled hen.

Greaves, the butler who opened the door, was about to tell her that the tradesmen's entrance was around the back, when Jenny blurted out:

'I've got somethin' very important to say about young Mr. Baldwin. Is they any of his family at home?'

'Step inside, Miss,' Greaves said. He did not want anyone to see him conversing with this strange specimen.

Jenny passed into the entrance hall. Greaves looked at her

as though she were a lump of mud that had been brought in on someone's shoes.

'Wait here,' he told Jenny, as he went to announce this strange visitor.

Greaves found Alice Baldwin in the library.

Alice had the chaste appearance of the born Puritan. Her strait-lacedness she inherited from her mother who died when Wayne was a small boy. She knew her father to be one of those free spirits who take their pleasure where they find it. And she feared that Wayne was very much like him.

She had heard persistent rumours of Wayne's affair with some beautiful blonde woman, who Alice suspected was a creature of the theatre, perhaps a chorus girl.

She looked up from her book as Greaves entered.

'There is a person here, madam,' said Greaves, 'who says she 'as something to say concerning Mr. Wayne. She says it's very important.'

Alice could tell from the way Greaves said the word 'person' that the caller was a questionable character. Her mind flashed to the blonde girl of Wayne's. Could this be she? Well, whoever it was, she would see her.

'She gave no name, Greaves?'

'No, madam.'

'Have her come in here.'

'Yes, madam.'

Alice laid her book on the library table and rose expectantly.

Cokey Jenny was shown in. She was wrapped in a long black coat with bedraggled fox collar. Underneath she wore a black gown which was modish but badly wrinkled and stained. Her pointed black satin slippers were spotted where she had spilt gin on them in Nigger Gert's. Powder and lip rouge were artfully applied, redeeming somewhat the hard lips and thick features. Her eyes were bright pinpoints of light, the pupils contracted by the effects of the dope she had taken. Vengeful pride flickered in their depths.

'You have something important to say?'

'Yeah,' said Jenny, 'about Mr. Wayne Baldwin.'

'Yes,' said Alice. 'My brother – what about him?'

'Ain't heard nothin' about this dame he's got, didja?'

Alice regarded the girl narrowly.

'No,' she said. 'I can't say that I have. I don't even know her name.'

Jenny's lips twisted bitterly.

'Well, I know it plenty. It's Babe Gordon.'

'Yes? You know something about her?'

'I'll say I do,' Jenny's voice rasped. 'I know her like nobody else.'

'What is she? An actress?'

Jenny laughed harshly.

'I'll say she's an actress. Not the kind on the stage. But nobody can beat her puttin' on her act wit' men.'

'What do you know about her?'

'She used to be a hooker around the Marathon Fight Club.'

'What do you mean by that?'

'She was just a common ordinary tart.'

'How do you know that?'

'I was one meself. Me an' her was pals.'

Alice recoiled before the coarse revelation.

'We got money from managers to play up to other managers' fighters. Get 'em drunk, before their fights – weaken 'em so's they would lose. And we'd try to pick the winners after a fight, because they copped the big end of the dough.'

Alice was startled and paled a little, but Jenny went right on, warming up to her subject like a college professor enthusiastically lecturing on organic biology. The revelations she made to Alice about Babe's professional activities, and her own, would have been shocking enough even to Alice's sophisticated brother. To the sister, the effect was overwhelming. Occasionally she had to ask for an explanation, for Cokey Jenny's highly technical language was just as strange to Alice as the deeds she described.

'Well, I'll tell you,' Jenny went on. 'You see, it like this . . . we goes out and rents a room in a hotel or a room in some house . . . ' More lurid details followed . . . 'O' course, these guys know what they're comin' for, they ain't never in the dark about that . . . ' She gave accurate descriptions . . . 'That's what we calls a quick turnover. Babe was great at that stuff . . . ' And so on.

Alice's clenched hands showed white at the knuckles.

'Where did your acquaintance with this Babe Gordon begin?'

'In the Harlem nigger joints.'

'Do you mean that her associations all her life have been with prizefighters and negroes?'

'Yeah, and dope pedlars. She peddled dope herself right in the Baldwin store in Harlem. Your brother got her out of the mess when she was caught.'

'I heard something about trouble up there.'

'Yeah,' said Jenny with a grin of malicious satisfaction. 'Before she went with your brother, she had a rich nigger lover. He's in gaol now, but he'll soon be out lookin' for her, an' if he catches her wit' your brother there'll be hell to pay. That's one of the reasons why I'm here. To tip youse off. An' youse don't like that kind of stuff in the newspapers. Especially to be mixed up wit' a nigger.'

Alice felt sick. She swayed slightly. Her hand sought the bell. Jenny saw the motion and got ready to go. 'Ain't this dame comin' across wit' a little dough, after me spillin' the dirt to her?' she thought, and lingered.

She wants money, Alice thought. But I had better not give her any. She might make a habit of coming here. Perhaps, later, I could give her something.

'Thank you,' she said. 'Thank you for telling me – everything.'

'You ain't gonna let this Babe Gordon make a mess of your brother's life, are ya?'

'I shall take what steps I think necessary,' said Alice.

Greaves appeared in the doorway.

'Yes, madam.'

'The young lady is going, Greaves.'

'Yes, madam.'

The next thing Jenny knew she was standing outside on the entrance steps, the door closed firmly behind her.

'Well, of all the cheap, lousy dames. Wort' millions an' she wouldn't even slip me a saw-buck, after me givin' her the low down. But I ain't finished wit' you, you yeller-haired Babe!'

21

THE BALDWINS

THE immediate effect upon Alice Baldwin of her scene with Cokey Jenny was a violent attack of hysterics. A little street-walker had come into her life and told her a tale which shook the Baldwin household to its foundations.

Never within the memory of living generations had there been a scandal associated with the Baldwin name. Now everything that name stood for was threatened by the outrageous conduct of her brother.

She would not have listened to Jenny a minute if she had not heard bits of gossip that connected Wayne with a mysterious blonde woman. She would have branded everything the obviously underworld creature told her as a lie – the beginning of a blackmail plot. But even before Jenny had told her all, Alice's intuition, coupled with what she had gleaned from her friends, warned her that the sordid revelations were undoubtedly true.

Her first thought after getting control of her shattered nerves was that she must employ every means possible to save her brother from exposure and disgrace. She had herself to consider, too, now that she was to become the wife of Jack Rathburne. His family meant as much as hers socially. Wayne was a young fool. She suspected that he had had mistresses when he was in Paris. That was well enough as long as he left them there. But to take up with a creature as utterly low and depraved as this Gordon woman was – oh, it was horrible!

She got her father on the phone at once and insisted that he come home right away. She told him that the matter was of the most vital importance to all of them.

Baldwin Senior, tall, silver-haired, distinguished, dropped everything at the office and hurried home. He came into the library with a worried look on his face. Alice sat limply in a chair, a handkerchief pressed against her lips. Her eyes blazed with a cold fury. She was ghastly pale.

'Why, good heavens, Alice, what is the matter?' her father inquired. 'You look ill.'

He went over and stood looking down on her.

'Father,' said Alice, 'I know you hate anyone to mince words with you. So I won't. Wayne has placed us in a dangerous position. All of us.'

'Dangerous position?' The elder Baldwin raised his eyebrows. 'Oh, come now, Alice, you have a habit of exaggerating things. What could Wayne possibly do to put us in such a position?'

'Wayne has a mistress,' said Alice coldly.

Her father's eyes widened and then he endeavoured to smother a smile that came unbidden to his lips.

'Oh, I know what you're thinking,' Alice said. 'There's nothing terrible in that. But this woman is the lowest person I have ever heard of. She is not only a former prostitute but only a few months ago she was the mistress of a wealthy negro in Harlem, who is now serving a gaol sentence.'

Her father stiffened as though struck full in the face. He moistened his lips.

'Is – is this true? I warn you, Alice, don't say these things if they are not true.'

'They are true, Father, I swear it!'

'Good God!' He sank into a chair and stared at the row of book-shelves.

155

'I have not told you the depths of her degeneracy. I have spared you that much, Father. We have got to do something, and at once.'

'Yes, yes, we must,' Baldwin said absently. 'But perhaps Wayne does not know what this woman is. We must tell him somehow. That will be the end of it, I'm sure.'

'Father,' said Alice, 'the easiest solution is to get him to accompany me to Europe. At once.'

'But he's just come home, my dear.'

'That doesn't make any difference. It is the only way out. If he remains in town he is bound to continue seeing this woman.'

'Perhaps you are right. We must try to persuade him that that is the best course.'

They were both startled when Wayne appeared in the doorway. He looked from one to the other.

'Hello,' he said, 'what's up? They told me at the office, Dad, that you left for home in a rush. They suspected something was the matter so I followed right after you.'

Baldwin Senior forced a smile.

'Alice made up her mind suddenly that she wants to go to Europe right away.'

Wayne smiled.

'What's the matter? Have a scrap with Jack?'

'No,' said Alice with a cold stare.

'Alice thought that you might go abroad with her.'

Wayne laughed.

'But I've just got back. Why doesn't Alice wait till she and Jack are married, and make the trip with him?'

'We've decided you had better go with her, Wayne.'

Wayne frowned in annoyance. There was something wrong here.

'I don't see the necessity of my going to Europe with Alice. There is plenty for me to do here.'

'Keeping that terrible woman amused, I suppose,' Alice said cuttingly.

Wayne flushed.

'What's that? What do you mean?'

'My boy,' said his father, 'we know you are involved with a woman. We have learned from reliable sources that she is an undesirable character, to say the least.'

Wayne hesitated. What did they know? Where had they secured any information?

'Well, yes,' he said, 'I admit that I'm very much interested in a certain young woman. There's no secret in that.'

'Perhaps not,' said Alice, 'but she seems to have kept certain secrets concerning her past from you very well.'

'Well, what of it? You've no business to intrude on my private life.'

Alice was bitterly sarcastic now.

'Your private life seems to be an open book. You appear to be one of very few who don't know that this girl you are so ready to defend is a former street-walker!'

'That's a lie!' he exploded. 'A damn lie! Whoever started that story is some blackmailer, and I can prove it!'

'Yes,' said Alice. 'I suppose you are fool enough to believe her in preference to facts.'

'You keep out of my affairs, do you hear? You can't control me like a puppet!'

Alice sneered coldly.

'This woman is not worthy of the exalted opinion you evidently honour her with.'

'Confound your puritanical meddling, Alice!'

Baldwin the elder turned a grave face toward his son. He spoke in businesslike tones.

'You had better get out of this affair, Wayne, and go abroad with your sister.'

'Wait a minute, Father,' Wayne cried. 'Alice has made some pretty raw statements. She'd better know what she's talking about.'

Her lips drew into a thin line.

'I think I know what I'm talking about, Wayne.' She rose and came determinedly before him. 'There's a low streak in you, Wayne, and you know it.'

Wayne half turned away and then wheeled back.

'There's nothing as low as the greed right here.' His voice hit a higher tone. 'My mother married my father for his gold bags and he bought her for her social label. We're all low; you cover your slime with virgin respectability. Thank God, I haven't your stinking Puritanical mind.'

'That will do, Wayne,' commanded Baldwin Senior. 'You're being insulting!'

But Wayne was carrying high the torch of his indignation.

'Where do you get your purity to question my morals? You're just a whited sepulchre.'

'Wayne!' his father cried.

Alice, cold with rage, said in biting tones, 'I think you should know, Father, that the low woman's name is Babe Gordon and that she seriously endangered your business by selling drugs in your Harlem store. You may remember the search made by detectives not so long ago. Wayne saved her from the police – for himself evidently.'

'It's a lie — '

'It is the truth, Father!'

Alice placed one hand on her father's shoulder.

'The Five and Ten Cent girl who worked behind the perfume counter in your Hundred and twenty-fifth Street Harlem store is also the gorgeous blonde Wayne has been keeping in luxury in Riverside Drive, I have positive proof!'

'You have no such proof!' Wayne shouted.

'I have. Irrefutable proof!'

'From whom?'

'From a person known as Cokey Jenny, who was the bosom companion of your fair Babe Gordon, when they solicited men on the streets!'

Wayne gave a hoarse laugh of derision.

'You believe that lying, blackmailing, gangster woman?'

'I have verified her statements. This Babe Gordon is an underworld seductress with criminal intent upon the Baldwin fortune. No one knows anything about her parentage. Whoever her parents were, they could not have been much to allow a girl of her age to be initiated into the vice and slime of Harlem. She has very likely inherited their miserable traits. I understand she carried on affairs with men when she was a mere schoolgirl. These are true facts.'

Wayne choked with a growing mortification.

'You've gone out of your head, Alice.'

Suddenly he felt ashamed in front of his father, who had said so little, but who had regarded him with a not unsympathetic look.

'Son,' his father's voice reached him, 'do you still refuse to go to Europe with Alice?'

Wayne raised his head.

'Why can't you be human and understanding where my feelings are concerned? Why can't you and Alice be tolerant of what I love?'

Alice's voice shot out like an arrow.

'Love? Sickening passion!'

Wayne shook his head hopelessly.

Alice worried him like a dog with a bone.

'She isn't expecting you to enter into the holy bond of matrimony, is she?'

Wayne faced them in a last stand.

'I'm demanding the right to love the object that makes for my peace of mind and soul, and I do not consider it any of your business.'

'My boy,' his father interrupted, in a kindly tone, 'whatever the colour of your views, the fact remains that a house divided against itself cannot stand. You are in the grip of a love affair that is shocking, particularly to your sister. Your enslavement to this woman is breaking down your loyalty to your family. Common sense demands that you give up this woman who is not worthy of your affection.'

'She is, I tell you, Father. She is!'

'Loving her, you are hardly an unbiased judge. The question is, will you leave her, and get your mind clear for business again?'

Wayne came to a final decision.

'No, Father, I'm bored stupid with the swank of our millions. My mind's made up. I want this girl who is just natural and normal, and I'm going to have her.'

A tomb-like silence filled the library for a moment, then Alice sarcastically flung at him,

'Then, Wayne, you've decided to defy common sense and disgrace your family for this *natural, normal* girl?'

'Yes – in spite of all the insults you heap on her.' He took a few steps, then turned with unseeing eyes. 'I'm going – I'm going,' he murmured as he swung out through the door.

Baldwin Senior and Alice faced each other in silence. His eyes dropped before her steady, unrelenting gaze.

'What are we to do now?' he asked helplessly.

A thin smile crossed Alice's face.

'Nothing,' she said. 'Nothing now. I have a premonition – just a premonition – that we shan't have to do anything.'

Wayne left his father's house with an intense loathing for all it represented. They had tried to make him feel like a bad little boy who needed a spanking. He resented the imputation that he was incapable of arranging his own life. They had besmirched Babe's character, and that hurt him the most. Try as he would to exonerate her, he was forced to admit that there must be some truth in what they had told him.

He knew when he had taken her as his mistress that she was no paragon of virtue. He had known about the negro, Money Johnson. But when he thought of her as a street-walker taking on the first corner, it made his flesh creep with revulsion. He wished he could sponge that thought from the slate of his mind. All he wanted was to enjoy Babe in peace. Why couldn't they let him be happy with the only woman who had ever completely satisfied him?

Wayne drove up to the Riverside Drive apartment. He let himself in with his own key. Babe was not in the living-room, but he found her, wearing a seductive négligé, sitting before the dressing-table in the bedroom. When he saw her he suddenly realized that undoubtedly some of the comments his family had made about her were true.

But even now when he was disillusioned her beauty struck him with such force that he was ready to forget her past. He wanted to lose himself completely in his love of her.

He crossed the room to Babe and, bending down, kissed her on the cheek. It was not the passionate kiss she was expecting, and she looked up at him, wondering what could be the matter. 'He looks a bit pale. Maybe it's just a headache or something. It'll pass off,' she thought as she continued arranging her hair.

Baldwin slipped into a lounging robe, and, lighting a cigarette, dropped into a chair by the window with an audible sigh. That sigh made Babe turn and look at him with an inquiring glance. He was so silent to-day.

She finished dressing, Baldwin watching her moving about the room without comment. More than half an hour passed in rather strained silence. Finally, Baldwin crushed his cigarette in the ash-stand at his elbow and leaned forward.

'You haven't heard from that girl Jenny lately, have you, sweetheart?'

'Why, she called up yesterday morning, Wayne,' said Babe, 'and I told her not to bother me any more, and told her that if she thought I would come across with any money, she was just out of her mind.'

'What kind of girl is she, dear?' Baldwin inquired. 'Have you known her very long? Is she just a liar and a trouble-maker?'

It began to dawn on Babe that these questions were leading up to something. She wondered if that 'low slut' Jenny had been telling him things.

Babe went over to him and kissed him.

'There is something worrying you, dear,' she said. 'I could see that when you came in. Tell me what it is.'

'There's no use in worrying you, sweetheart, with my troubles.'

Babe stroked his hair.

'Oh, but you'll feel better if you tell me. If it's trouble, share it with me. I want to help you, Wayne dear.'

Baldwin hesitated. He had never lied to Babe; perhaps it would be better to tell her, as gently as he could.

'That girl Jenny,' he began, 'has been causing a lot of trouble again.'

Babe feigned surprise.

'No! How?'

'Why – why, she has gone to my sister and lied – lied about you!'

'About me?'

'Yes. She said vile things about you, dear. Terrible things. And what makes it so damn rotten is that my father and sister believe her.'

He told her some of what Jenny had revealed, but he omitted the part about Babe's being a street-walker, and did not mention Money Johnson.

Babe placed her arms around his neck.

'Oh, Wayne,' she said, 'what a terrible, dangerous creature Jenny is. She thinks nothing of ruining my reputation, of destroying our happiness. But you don't believe these things!'

Again under the influence of Babe's charm, intoxicated with the perfume of her body, Baldwin truthfully replied:

'No, I know you too well, darling, to believe anything like that.'

'Do your people want you to give me up?'

'Yes. But of course I refused. I tried to convince them that they were all wrong. I told them I wouldn't give you up no matter what happened!'

He held her closely in his arms and buried his face in her bosom. She laughed and mussed up his hair. Lifting his head he kissed her full lips until she could hardly breathe. Everything to him was the same as before. She was his, and to hell with the rest of the world.

Jenny, of course, was still a dangerous factor, but she could be dealt with in several ways. She was a drug addict, and could be sent away. People should be protected against that type of woman. But he did not want to be responsible for sending anyone to gaol. Perhaps when she learned that her scheme to get even with Babe had failed, she would cease to trouble them.

Then the thought of Babe's husband popped into his head; perhaps he, too, might want to cause trouble. He wondered if this prizefighter husband would turn up. Not that he was afraid of anyone. But there were the newspapers ready to pounce on any bit of scandal that promised juicy reading.

'Have you heard anything from your husband?' Baldwin asked Babe.

'No,' said Babe, 'but he ought to be home any day now. He's been away more than three months.'

Babe wondered at his question, because Baldwin had never spoken of marriage, although he had mentioned something about her divorcing the Bearcat.

'You must free yourself from him, dear, as soon as he comes back. He might make trouble if he finds out about our living together. Is he the kind that would listen to reason, if I backed it up with a substantial financial settlement?'

'Let me handle him, Wayne,' said Babe. 'I know his ways.'

His months of training had put the Bearcat in the pink of condition again. Babe had written him a few encouraging letters, and with the cheerful, easy-going Joe Malone as a companion, his life in the camp was quite happy, except that he missed Babe.

Charlie Yates had come up to the camp with a new boy he was training, and received the surprise of his life when he saw the Bearcat wade through his boxing partners, and then step out for a ten-mile hike.

'What a great fighter I missed havin' in him!' Charlie told himself with a feeling of regret.

He and the Bearcat became friends again through the good-natured manœuvring of Joe Malone. Charlie still liked the kid, anyway.

Joe even persuaded Charlie to arrange a match for the Bearcat on his return. If he made good Charlie had other bouts in mind for him. He began to have real respect for the Bearcat, now that he had torn himself away from that no-good dame of his. Charlie had heard about Babe's being with Money Johnson and, assuming the Bearcat had heard it too, thought the fighter was well out of her clutches.

The Bearcat was grateful to Charlie, and he returned to New York with fresh energy, and a determination to make good for Babe's sake.

22

THE HOUSE OF ALL NATIONS

Money Johnson bore no resentment toward those who had plotted his downfall. It was all in the racket. He had grabbed off too much to suit the other sporting interests in Harlem, so friends gave him the tip that he could expect trouble when he got out of stir. The opposition was sore that he was locked up for only three months. They had hoped for at least a year, confident that if he were away for that length of time they could destroy his business and prestige in Harlem. But Johnson was a clever negro. He had lieutenants he could trust, who looked after his interests while he was in gaol.

What really disturbed him most was the loss of his white woman. Three months without her were torture for him. He didn't mind the gaol so much. It was the thought of losing Babe that nearly drove him insane. Those three months dragged out like thirty years.

He was soon to learn about Babe. Willis, a friend of his, who was a waiter in the Harley Club, visited Johnson in his cell. After they had talked for a few minutes, Willis said:

'Money, Ah think Ah done see yo' woman, las' night.'

Money's eyes flashed.

'Yo' mean yo' done see Babe?'

'Ah think so.'

'Tell me, man – tell me where yo' see her?'

'Up at duh club. Ah was waitin' on her – Ah knows dat pretty face o' hers when Ah sees it.'

'Whut she doin' dere? Who was she wit'?' Johnson cried excitedly.

'She was wit' a young gen'leman name' Baldwin. He son o' duh man what owns all dem Five an' Tens.'

'Whut he say to her? Whut he say?'

'Ah don' know what he say. He seem pow'ful crazy 'bout her, do'!'

Johnson paced furiously up and down his cell. He turned to Willis.

'Yo' try an' find out fo' me where at she is stayin', Willis, yo' heah?'

'Ah don' know, but Ah'll try to find out fo' yo', Money.'

Johnson was in a sweat of impatience until he was released from gaol the following day. His car was waiting for him and he was driven to his place on Strivers' Row. Although he was dying for some decent food, a big meal of fried chicken that was awaiting his arrival remained untasted.

Six of his henchmen, who managed his various places, were in his apartment waiting to make reports.

They greeted him with slaps on the back and hearty hand-shakes. But Johnson broke loose from them and stormed up and down the room.

'Go git mah woman!' he cried. 'Go an' git her, Ah tells ya! Ah gotta have mah woman!'

One of his lieutenants cried:

'Lord, man, sit down, yo' ain't in gaol-house now! Man, sit down an' eat somepin'.'

'Ah don' want nothin' to eat. Ah want mah woman! Where is she at? Where is dey hidin' her?'

'Nobody's hidin' her,' said another. 'She mus' be some place aroun'. Don' get yo'self all bothered! We got a lot to tell yo'. Ever' one o' us here been gittin nothin' but trouble fum duh police since yo' been gone.'

'Ah don' care nothin' about nothin'. Ah got to git mah woman back, yo' heah!' Johnson was working himself up to fever pitch. 'Git her fo' me, Ah says, goddam it!' He snatched up a Louis XV chair and smashed it into kindling against the wall.

The others drew back in alarm. Johnson could be bad when he was worked up.

'Aw right! Aw right! We try to find her fo' yo'. We puts our ears to duh groun' and tries to find her fo' yo'.'

The next day, after a bad night, during which he tried to console himself with a load of gin, Johnson heard about Babe. Again it was Pearl, Babe's maid, who was the source of information. She agreed to give Babe a note from Money Johnson.

Johnson had arranged for a hideway before he left gaol. He could not remain in Strivers' Row, for the cops would keep a strict watch on him. Right now they were watching every joint he owned, waiting for an excuse to close them up.

He knew if he brought Babe to Strivers' Row it would surely spell trouble, and he had seen enough of the inside of a prison for a while.

Babe read Johnson's note with a feeling of trepidation. She did not want to be mixed up with him again. She was perfectly contented with her present life. Still, it might be advisable to see Johnson just once to close the episode. Besides, Pearl was persuasive. She had learned of Babe's affair with Money Johnson, and she knew he could be desperate. It would be better for her mistress to go and see him and sort of let him down easy like.

'Ah knows yo' don' care 'bout Money Johnson, Mis' Babe,' Pearl told her, 'but he'd die fo' yo'. Jus' go an' see him once – jus' once anyway. Ah knows yo' don' care about him. But Ah knows how Ah'd feel ef Ah had a white man an' he done lef' me. But, good Lawd, Ah's too ugly to have a white man.

Hard enough fo' me to git a coloured man. Mis' Babe, please go to him ef only fo' a little while.'

It was early afternoon, and Babe decided that if she went to see Johnson she'd be back in time for dinner. Hurrying into her street clothes she called a taxi, and was driven to Johnson's home in Strivers' Row. Here she was met by two friends of Money's who guided her to the apartment where the big negro had taken to cover.

This hideaway was a railway flat in a four-story tenement with two flats to each floor. The apartment Johnson occupied was on the second floor of this building to the right. Two bootlegger friends had turned it over to him. It was more comfortably furnished than any of the other flats in the house.

But Johnson would never have chosen this place as a hideaway, much less have invited Babe to come there, had he known that Big Ida, a negro stick-up woman, and one of his cast-off flames, lived in a flat on the top floor.

Ida had been Johnson's sweetheart – that is, one of them – in his lean days. And though he had long ago discarded her, this gigantic wench believed that no one but the white woman, Babe Gordon, could have kept him from coming back to her.

She was sitting in her parlour window with the shutter partly open to get a breath of air, when, looking down, she saw a motor-car pull up in front of the building. Two men got out. Their faces were familiar to her; she knew them as Pinhead Pete and Liverlips Sam, henchmen of Money Johnson.

'Lawd!' Ida muttered to herself. 'Whut's dem niggers doin' roun' here? Dey looks respicious, too.'

The two men in question looked up and down the block and then Pinhead entered the house. Ida watched and wondered. Liverlips was leaning into the car talking to someone. Then in a minute or two Pinhead came down. He seemed to indicate that everything was all right – that the coast was clear. The door of the sedan opened and a tall negro got out.

Big Ida's eyes opened wide.

'Money Johnson!' she exclaimed under her breath. 'Whut's he doin' here!' A faint hope stirred in her massive bosom. 'He ain't a-comin' to see me, is he?'

She sprang up and rushed through the door leading from the parlour to the hall. Down the well of the stairs she could see Johnson and his companions coming up. But they stopped on the second floor, and she heard a door close after them.

Ida shook her head.

'Ah might a' knowed he wasn't comin' up to me, duh dirty, sneakin' nigger!'

With unbelievable ease she moved her great weight silently down the old stairs, and at the second floor she paused. She heard men's voices on the right of the hall. She listened close to the door. She distinguished Money's deep voice. Satisfied that she knew where he was and highly excited at the presence of her old love, Big Ida went rapidly down the remaining flight of steps to the first floor and burst into old Liza Jones' flat to the right of the entrance, perspiration pouring down every inch of her large body.

Old Liza was a sprightly coloured woman with a mass of kinky grey hair. Her face for all her age still possessed something of the good looks of her youth. She had worked as a maid in a high-class white hook-shop in the Tenderloin, remaining there until District Attorney Jerome had cleaned up the city. Now she was the janitress of this flat-house.

When Big Ida bounced into her flat Liza was just about to go out, but seeing that something was wrong she inquired:

'What's duh matter wid ya, honey? Yo' looks worri'd!'

Ida sat down by the window in Liza's parlour.

'Lawd, Liza,' Ida said. 'Ah jes' seed mah man come in heah.'

Liza appeared mildly surprised.

'Well, whut youse frettin' about, chile? Ain't yo' glad to see him?' Ida moaned.

'Lawd, he don' wan' nothin' t' do wid me. He done t'rew me down.'

She looked out of the widow and Pinhead and Liverlips came out on the front stoop, descended and got into the sedan at the kerb.

'Dere goes two o' Money's boys,' Ida said. 'He mus' be stayin' up dere.'

'Yo' mean Money Johnson's upstairs? Ah thought he was in duh gaol-house.'

'Yeah, but he out agin now. Ah don' know whut he doin' heah, 'cept he's hidin' or somepin'.'

Across the hall, in the flat opposite, they heard the Filipino hat-maker cursing his wife, a Porto Rican negress who swore back in Spanish, French, and English.

'Lawd 'a' mercy!' said Liza Jones. 'Ah ain't never heard such outlandish langwidge as dem two shoutin'. She sho' make hell-fire wid dat mout' o' hern!'

But Ida wasn't interested in other people's troubles. She had dark suspicious thoughts of her own. With her chin resting on the palm of her big black hand which was pink on the inside, her hot smoky eyes looked restlessly up and down the street. Then she turned suddenly to Liza Jones.

'Ah'm nervouser dan a mule wid duh itch, Liza. Has yo' got gin in duh house?'

Liza went to a closet and produced a bottle of gin. She poured a stiff drink for Ida and a smaller one for herself.

Big Ida, who was continually looking out of the window, suddenly stiffened. The sedan she had seen before was back again and was stopping in front of the house. She could see Liverlips at the wheel. Pinhead opened the rear door when the car drew to the kerb. A white woman, dressed very plainly, got out. She turned to Pinhead, who appeared to give her directions. Then he sprang back in the car and drove off.

Ida got a glimpse of the face and blonde hair of the woman. Very quickly the visitor was up the steps and into the vestibule. Ida leapt up with an oath and rushed to open Liza's parlour door into the hall. But by the time she had it open, the white woman was half-way up the first flight of stairs. Ida, breathing heavily, her nostrils distended, her hands clutching spasmodically, watched where she went. Yes – the woman was going right to Money Johnson. Ida swung back into Liza's parlour, her lips drawn back to an ugly snarl, revealing two tarnished gold teeth.

'Ah knows it was dat dirty white trash! Yes, she's up dere now. She's up dere wid dat man. Lawd hab mercy on her soul, 'cause Ah'll snatch duh eyes outen her head!'

Big Ida ranted up and down the parlour. Liza watched her with growing apprehension. She knew that Ida was like when she was aroused.

'Look yere, woman,' Liza Jones said to her, 'whutcha goin' on like dat fo'? Actin' lak a mad baboon!'

Ida whipped up her skirt above her right knee and slipped a black-jack from out of her garter. She swung it in the air viciously, as though striking some imaginary victim. The force of her mighty, muscular shoulders was behind each blow. Liza got out of the way.

'Why did Ah let dat slut git pass me?'

Liza edged into a corner of the room.

'Hushup wid dat lowdown talk an' put dat head-buster away. Ah's scared o' dem t'ings anyway.'

Ida paused as she saw the gin bottle, and held it to her lips while the hot liquid poured down her throat.

'Oh,' she moaned then, 'what'll Ah do? What'll Ah do? She up dere wid mah man now. Oh, she's wid mah man!'

Liza took the gin bottle and locked it in the closet.

'Who's up dere wid yo' man?' she asked. 'Whutcha all takin' on about, woman?'

After some minutes, Liza succeeded in calming Ida down.

But Ida dragged a chair up by the hall door and sat with the door ajar, watching the stairs, waiting for Babe to come down. She laid the blackjack in her lap and every once in a while she'd pick it up and make wild passes at an imaginary foe, or else caress its leaden head affectionately.

Money Johnson had been watching for Babe, and at her knock he opened the door of the flat immediately. He forgot for a moment what Willis had told him about her dining in some club with a handsome white man.

The three months in the gaol-house had told on him. He grabbed Babe in his arms like a savage and started kissing her. It all happened so quickly that Babe could hardly get her breath. She wasn't exactly in the mood for this sort of love-making.

She had become quite used to Baldwin's more sophisticated brand of passion. And she had lost her interest in this big dinge. Yes – it was just too bad that he had to carry on this way.

'What's the idea of bringin' me to this dump?' Babe snapped at him.

Johnson was taken aback.

'Why, honey, this is just a little hideaway o' mine, where Ah can have mah baby to mahself. Oh, how Ah wanted yo'. In dat mean ol' gaol-house Ah couldn't sleep nights thinkin' about yo'. Oh, honey, how I missed messin' round with you.'

He glanced down at her as he said it and noticed she had too many clothes on to suit him.

'Come on, take all dese dresses of. Take dat stuff off.'

Babe pushed him away.

'I can only stay a little while, Money. I got to go.'

She stood up and went over to the dressing-table and powdered her nose in the mirror. 'My God! The way I look! You've got me lookin' a sight. Just look at my hair. Look at the lip-rouge all over my face. Get me a towel, hurry!'

She took his breath away. He could see in her eyes that she was cold and disgusted with him. Then what Willis had told him about the handsome white man was true. 'She's got somebody new! She's tired o' me!' He knew that look in her face, for he knew how he had looked at his women when he was tired of them. He had been cruel and rotten to them and now he was getting a taste of his own medicine.

Babe saw him staring at her in the mirror. She turned around in a flash.

'What the hell are you lookin' at? Go get me that towel!'

He wasn't used to these tones from her or anyone else. Money Johnson had never been a servant. Yet unconsciously he walked over, picked up a towel and handed it to her.

She snatched it roughly from his hand and started wiping her face with it. Then with some highly perfumed powder and lip-stick she restored the perfection of her appearance, and turned from the mirror with an expression changed from crossness to one of self-approval.

'Where's my hat?' she demanded.

It had fallen to the floor when he had first seized her.

His heart sank as he saw that she preparing to go.

'What are yo' doin' to me? What are yo' treatin' me like this fo'?'

'What do you mean?' Babe said coldly.

'Wantin' to go an' leavin' me like this.' His eyes had the look of a hurt animal.

'I'm sorry, I've got to get downtown; I've got something important to attend to. I really shouldn't have come up here to-day. But I was anxious to see you. I thought I'd come here and stay a little while and go. I can come back again to-morrow. Then maybe I can stay here with you.'

'What yo' got to do dat's mo' important dan me?' He knew she was lying – just trying to get away.

As she stood looking at him, she couldn't think of any reason she could tell him for wanting to go.

As he sat down on the arm of a chair, his flashy robe, which was not buttoned but tied at the waist with a silk cord, fell open.

Babe hesitated a moment; her eyes travelled over his symmetrical body. Finally her eyes met his. They were both thinking. Babe thought: 'Oh, what the hell. A couple of hours won't hurt.' She picked up a cigarette and Johnson quickly lit a match and held it for her.

'Get me a drink!' she commanded.

He poured her a whisky straight, and she drank it down. He also had one.

Then he went over to her.

'Ah knows yo' wouldn't leave me. Ah knows yo' couldn't leave me, when yo' know how much Ah wantcha.'

He held her in his arms and kissed her. They stood in front of the mirror on the dressing-table.

He looked in the mirror. Then he said: 'Look in dere. Don't dat make yo' think o' somepin'?'

His hand started moving down her arms, fingering her black lace dress.

'Take dis here thing off,' he cried. 'Ah jus' can't stand it. Ah'm jus' goin' to lose mah mind, that's all.'

Over in the next flat, Fat Tess was playing a low-down record that was strangely appropriate to the moment:

Honey baby, won't you cuddle near.
Let sweet papa whisper in your ear.
I'm wild about that thing, it makes me laugh and sing.
Give it to me, mama, I'm wild about that thing.

Wild about it when you hold me tight.
Let me linger in your arms all night.
I'm wild about that thing, my passion's got to fling.
Can't you hear me cryin', I'm wild about that thing.*

---

* This song is copyright 1929 by Georgia Music Co., to whom thanks are due for permission to print the above verses.

'Oh, baby, yo' hear dat?' cried Johnson. 'Ah'm wild about dat thing!'

He intended to keep her there. Never to let her out of his sight. She couldn't go back to the other man now. If things got too hot for him here, he figured on going to Paris with her where black and white could live openly.

Yes – he'd be her slave for life. She could be cruel to him – beat him, kick him, treat him like a dog, but just let him love her.

Afternoon passed into evening, and then night, but still Babe did not come down, and still Big Ida waited in the dark parlour with the door ajar and her black-jack handy.

Liza sat by her and together they drank gin, the old woman growing mellow as the hours went by. She began reminiscing of the old days she had known. She drew from her experience pictures of things which she connected with what was going on upstairs.

'Yes, chile,' she told Ida, 'Ah seed duh white and duh black mixin' jus lak now. Duh coloured gals and duh white men and duh white gals and duh coloured men. Duh mixin' o' duh black an' white been goin' on fo' ages an' ages. Yo' read 'bout dat way back in duh Bible. Yes, chile, it's right dere in duh Good Book.'

Big Ida grunted and took another swig of gin. She didn't care much about Liza's philosophy. All the philosophy she wanted was contained in that loaded leather club that lay in her lap.

Liza rambled on, rocking back and forth in rhythmic time to her romantic recollections.

'Yes, ol' Liza sho' knows life. Had a heap o' experience.' From up above came the sound of a man and a woman moving about, the old boards of the building echoing every step. Then there was silence and from right over the heads of the watchers came the creaking of a chair. Liza cocked her head to one side and listened for a moment. Her lips twisted into a grin in the darkness.

'Dat man up dere,' she said, 'after bein' in gaol for three months, is feelin' lively.'

'Shut yo' mout', Liza, goddam yo'!' Big Ida growled. 'Ain't Ah busted up enough inside widout yo' remindin' me about dat low slut up dere?'

Liza grinned to herself.

'Lawd, chile, don' Ah know what's what? Ah ain't been workin' aroun' a hook-shop so long widout knowin' ever' little sound 'n' whut it means.'

'Yo's a great help to me now, yo' ol' witch! Whutcha paintin' dese goddam pitchers fo' anyhow? Yo' jus' drivin' me t' go upstairs an' bust dat door ef yo' keep it up.'

But Liza was too lost in her dreams to pay attention to Ida's objections.

'Yes, Ah use t' work in a high-class call-house until dat district attorney man close 'em all up. He jus' t'rew me outen a good job. Den Ah got to be a kep' woman mahself. Ol' Jonesy come along an' Ah took up wid him an' started livin' wid him. He had plenty o' money den. Ah was a pretty good-lookin' gal in mah day.'

But Ida began to get a trifle tired of old Liza Jones' bragging about how well kept she had been.

'Take yo' withered gums to bed, Liza, an' stop dis yere fabricatin'.'

But Liza droned on; she was like a swarm of locusts, there was no stopping her when she got started under the impetus of gin.

'Didn' Ah see dat Money Johnson? Lawd, he's a good-lookin' nigger. Ah don' blame yo', Ida. Ah knows Ah'd fight fo' mah man. Old Jonesy was a good man himself. 'Course he didn't hab no money lak Johnson. But money ain't ever'thin' – 'course it's quite a lot – but not ever'thin'. Yes, chile, Jonesy was pretty good in his day.'

And so the night wore on. Liza finally rolled off to bed. At seven o'clock she got up and discovered that Big Ida had dropped off to sleep in the chair. She covered her up with a blanket and went into the kitchen to make some breakfast.

At eight o'clock, Ida woke up with a start. She sprang up.

'Liza! Liza! She ain't done gone, is she? She ain't got away on me?'

'C'am yo'self, c'am yo'self, woman! Eveybody's still sleepin'.'

Ida sat down and ate some breakfast rapidly, then she returned to her post at the parlour door. After a while she heard footsteps up above. She could distinguish the short quick steps of a woman and the heavy footfall of a man. She drew a sigh of relief. Presently her frayed nerves began to demand a stimulant, and a search of the closet revealed no more gin.

She sat down again and waited. About noon her system cried so hungrily for alcohol that she literally flew at Liza's telephone. There were only two telephones in the whole house – Liza's, and one in the bootleggers' flat now occupied by Johnson.

She called Nigger Gert's. Gert answered the phone. Ida started in raving.

'Dis you, Gert? Dis is Ida. Oh, Lawd, Gert, sen' me some gin. Ah gotta hab gin!'

'Whut's duh matter wid yo', Ida?' Gert wanted to know.

'Hurry up dere, Gert – sen' me over a load o' gin!'

'Yo' gone crazy, woman? Talkin' wild lak dat over a little gin!'

'Ne' mind, git dat gin over here quick, yo' heah?'

'Ah'll git it over dere quick as Ah kin. Cain't git it no quicker. What yo' all excitin' fo'? Neber heard anyone gittin' dat excited 'bout likker.'

Ida's voice rose into a wail.

'Oh, duh dirty slut!'

'Look yere, woman, who yo' callin' a dirty slut?' Gert shouted into the 'phone.

'Ah'll cut her throat!'

'Whose throat yo' goin' to cut dere, woman? Who yo' talkin' about? Yo' won't do no cuttin'!'

'Ah don' mean yo' throat, Gert.'

'Bet yo' sweet life yo' don' mean mah throat!'

'Ah'll whittle her down.'

'Who yo' all talkin' about?'

'Oh, she's here!'

'Who dere?'

'Oh, dat lowdown oafy slut! She's here wid mah man!'

A number of the girls who were at Gert's, including Cokey Jenny, were attracted by Gert's end of the conversation on the phone.

'What man yo' talkin' 'bout, Ida?' Gert asked her.

'Mah man – Money Johnson – what man yo' think?'

Gert laughed.

'Why he's ever'body's man, woman!'

'Oh, Gert, duh Lawd done answered mah prayer. He done sent bof o' dem here. Hurry up wid dat gin.'

Ida hung up.

Gert turned away from the phone and shook her head.

'Dat woman' lak to go out o' her mind.'

'Who was dat, Gert?' inquired one of the girls curiously.

'Big Ida. She say Money Johnson an' his white trash is over dere. She jus' lak to kill duh bof o' dem Ah 'spect. She'll cut dat gal so many times she'll think she's a slot-machine. Ah cain't be bothered wid dese yere killin's, dese yere insides and outsides and nerpicides and suicides. Ah'm a business woman and Ah got to make money. Ah got rent to pay. Gotta be careful o' telephone talk. Git me in trouble.'

One of the girls laughed harshly.

'Ah, yo' make me sick about dis ol' joint o' yours.'

Gert was indignant.

'Look yere, woman, don't yo' go callin' dis yere dump a joint!'

Cokey Jenny eased over to Nigger Gert.

'What's the trouble, Gert? Did she really say Babe and Money Johnson is at her place and there's goin' to be trouble?'

Gert shrugged her shoulders.

'Nothin' but trouble! Nothin' but trouble!'

'That big nigger Ida'll kill that dame sure'n hell,' Jenny said to herself. 'Well, she's in for it now, the dirty louse. I'll take the gin over myself; it'll be a good excuse for me to go there. I don't want to miss none of it.'

Ida had resumed her station at the door. As she watched, a steady stream of men went up the stairs to the second floor to the flat opposite the one Johnson was in. It was occupied by a high-yellow, heavy-built and answering to the name of Fat Tess. Ida called Liza's attention to the parade of men.

Liza laughed.

'Business is good. See her out in a few days flashin' some fancy clo'es. She seems mighty popular. Ah see dem come often. Yo'd think dey was callin' on duh President. Just comin' in t' shake hands 'n' go out agin'.'

Money Johnson, too, had heard the footsteps of the callers at Fat Tess's flat and knew what was going on.

'Poor low niggers,' he thought, 'wit' one black woman. Ah's duh king. Got duh beautiful white woman all to mahself, when Ah wants an' all Ah wants.'

His mind flashed back to the days when he had five and six hustlers like Tess working for him. Johnson felt like grabbin' a smoke, so he called up Pinhead Pete to come over. Pinhead was one of the best 'chefs' in Harlem.

Pinhead arrived and cooked the little pills of gum-opium for Johnson and Babe, and the afternoon hours wore on. Pinhead burned a heavy incense to smother the fumes of the drug. Ida had seen Pete go in, and now when the odour of incense was wafted down to her she knew that he was 'cheffing' for Money Johnson, as he had done many times before.

'Dey're layin' duh hip,' she said to herself. 'Dey'll be good fo' five or six hours anyway. Guess Ah'll git me some sleep on Liza's bed.' As she turned away she heard a rumpus on the front stoop, and went to the window.

From the window of the top floor flat next to Ida's, where a Chinese laundryman lived with his black wife, a thin stream of water fell upon the Madame Walker kink-free marcel of a coloured housewife, who stood on the stoop. She started shouting imprecations as the water hit her head.

'Hey, you up dere, what ail you anyway?'

A huge black bust protruded from the upper window.

'Whut y'all shoutin' about? Guess Ah kin water mah jewraniums ef Ah wants to widout no permit from yo'.'

'Yo' don' understand me right 'bout lettin' dat flood drop over me. Ah's coming' up dere an' operate on yo' ear!'

A china platter came crashing down on the Madame Walker coiffure. The victim let out a yell and dashed into the house. She went screaming up the stairs to her flat on the third floor to apply arnica to her bruised head. In the apartment opposite hers, the door was open and several black hands holding cards could be seen around the table. The shutters of the room were closed to the day-light and electric lights were going full glare. Elsie, a young mulatto, lived here with her blue-black husband who now lay in a corner in a drunken sleep with his head in a cuspidor. The men had been playing cards and drinking all night. Elsie, lying in bed in the same room, suddenly shrieked at them.

'For Gawd's sake, turn off some o' dat light! Ah ain't keepin' company wid Edison!'

Ida was about to leave the window to go and lie down for a while, but she saw Cokey Jenny coming along the street. She packed her nostrils with snuff, while she waited for Jenny to reach the house. When Jenny entered the hall, Ida dashed out and dragged her into the flat.

'Come yere, come yere! Yo' knows who's heah? Right heah under mah very nose? Yo' gwine to drop off when yo' hear.'

Jenny pretended to be surprised. 'You mean — '

'Das who, das who. Parkin' wid Money Johnson, dat's whut dat mess o' sin doin'.'

Ida paced up and down the room with Jenny.

'Ah let her go in, but Ah'm gonna git her when she comes out. Ah been waitin' all night fo' her to bust her tripe outen dat door.' Ida went out in the hall and looked up to the next floor. She came back in the room. 'Dey's layin' duh hip up dere. But Ah ain't takin' no chances o' her 'scapin' me. Ah's just goin' to ruin' dat pretty face o' hers.'

A gloating leer pulled at Jenny's mouth. 'Don't be no damn fool. Money Johnson would break you up and throw you in the Harlem river. He'd know who done it. You stay right here and don't do nothin' but just what you're doin'.'

'Don't expect me to keep mah han's offen her, does ya?'

'Bustin' her up ain't goin' to get you nothin' but the work-house. Just watch her like you're doin' and ring me at Gert's whatever you find out, ya hear?'

'Don't see how she's goin' to git ruined dat way,' said Ida dubiously.

'She'll get plenty, if you do as I tell you,' said Jenny meaningly. 'You'll get yourself some dough too. Now you just watch me. I do things scientific. Use your head. It ain't smart to use your hands.'

'Yo' can't think when dey takes yo' man away fum yo'. It ain't so bad when dey takes yo' man's money away fum yo', but when some dirty low tripe takes yo' man's heart fum yo', dat's when it hurts.'

Liza opened the gin Jenny had bought over.

'Yere. Take a drink o' dis stuff an' pull yo'self togedder.'

Jenny went to Liza's phone and called the number to Babe's apartment in Riverside Drive. Pearl answered. Jenny asked if Babe were in, to find out what they knew about her. The maid said Miss Gordon was out.

Jenny hung up and turned to Ida.

'You don't need to worry. She'll be here a long time yet.'

Jenny then called Baldwin's office, but he had just left.

23

JENNY'S DOUBLE-PLAY

IT was about seven-thirty that evening when Cokey Jenny ran across the Bearcat. The meeting was accidental but Jenny never missed a trick.

The Bearcat was sitting in his cab, where he was parked near the subway entrance at 125th Street and Broadway. He was keeping up his training during the mornings. In the late afternoon and early evening he operated his taxi. He had won his fight with Red Dorgan, the fighter Charlie had matched him with, and was staging a sensational comeback. Nevertheless he was worried over the disappearance of Babe.

When he reached New York after his months in the mountains he went at once to the Five and Ten in Harlem and there learned that Babe had been out of the place for some time. He searched all over Harlem for her, watching the various resorts that Babe had once frequented, but he saw nothing of her. He did not give up hope, though, but ran his cab whenever possible in the Harlem district, feeling that sooner or later he would run across her.

Now Jenny saw him and hurried up to him. She could hardly wait to tell him where he could find his wife.

'Hello, Bearcat,' she greeted him.

'Hello,' he said, surprised at seeing Jenny. 'Where'd you come from?'

'Just come from a place where your wife is.'

'What!' The Bearcat almost leapt out of his seat. 'You just seen Babe? Where is she, Jenny? Tell me – where is she?'

Jenny's mouth twisted in a vicious grin.

'Why, you'll find her up at 127th West Street, near Lenox Avenue. She's — '

But Jenny didn't get a chance to say more, because the Bearcat threw his motor in gear and was off around the corner.

When the Bearcat arrived in 127th Street he remembered that in his excitement he had forgotten to get from Jenny the number of the house. But he saw the disreputable-looking row of houses and felt sure that Babe was in one of them, so he parked his car on the corner where he could watch for her.

Jenny was not satisfied with this bit of dirty work. She wasn't finished yet. From a booth, she continued her search for Baldwin over the phone. She called his father's house, and when she was told there that she might be able to locate him at one of four clubs, she called up each in turn but still could not him. Then she tried Babe's apartment again. The maid told her that Mr. Baldwin was there. Jenny did not wait to talk to him. She hung up and started across town to Riverside Drive.

Wayne Baldwin had waited up all the previous night for Babe to come home. The maid had professed ignorance of where Babe had gone. Wayne grew almost frantic as the morning hours arrived and she did not return. He decided to wait until night, and if she were not back then he would get a private detective agency on the job.

At first, he feared that she might have left him for good. But when he saw that all her fine clothes and her jewellery were in the apartment, he thought that she had met with some accident.

Just before Jenny had called, he began to look through

Babe's things, hoping that they might reveal some clue as to her whereabouts. In her trunk he was surprised to find a loaded automatic pistol. He wondered what she had ever carried that thing around for. He did not know that it had belonged to the Bearcat, who had taken the weapon out on a permit when he was still driving a truck. When Babe had packed up and left the Bearcat, she had picked up the gun among other things and tossed it into her trunk.

He found nothing that would give any clue to her disappearance. Babe had destroyed her note from Money Johnson. He paced up and down the apartment in a sweat of foreboding. The pile of cigarette-butts in the ash-trays became mountainous, still she did not return.

Jenny arrived at the apartment house and phoned up from the reception hall. Baldwin jumped when the phone rang, hoping against hope that it might be Babe. Jenny's voice greeted him.

'Mr. Baldwin?'

'Yes – speaking!'

'I'm calling from downstairs. This is Jenny. I got some information for you, if you'll see me.'

'All right, all right,' said Baldwin. 'I'll come down at once.'

When he came out of the lift into the lobby, there was no one there. 'Wonder where she is?' he thought. He walked out to the street, and, lighting a cigarette, he strolled toward the corner. A girl was standing there. It was growing dusk now and he wasn't sure he knew her. When he drew near, however, she spoke.

'I'm Jenny. You don't remember me, do you? I got some information for you!'

He was glad it was growing dark, for he didn't relish being seen talking to this tough character, although Jenny did not look half bad to-night. She wasn't dressed as gaudily as usual.

'Yes,' he said to her. 'What is it?'

Jenny's face took on a pleading look.

'I know I was a little wrong in tryin' to mix things up at your store and I thought maybe I could come around to-night and square things up.' Her look grew more sympathetic. "Cause deep down in my heart I likes Babe an' I heard lots o' nice things about you.'

Baldwin was impatient.

'Yes – yes. Do you know where she is?' He wasn't anxious for a long conversation with this person. He merely wanted information.

'Well, that's it,' Jenny said. 'I know where she is. I want to do you a good turn now.'

From her bag she drew a slip of paper and handed it to him.

'Here's where you can find her. That big nigger is bad when he drinks, and I don't want nothin' to happen to her. Of course, this information might not be worth anythin' to you, but again it might. I tried to get you all day.'

Baldwin knew what she was hinting at. He drew a sheaf of bills from his wallet, selected a fifty-dollar bill and handed it to her.

'Here, this may help a bit. Thank you for letting me know.'

Jenny took the bill, and told Baldwin the rest of the story. She looked at the bill in the dim light of the evening. 'Well,' she said to herself, 'it ain't so bad. It's better than nothin'. Now I'll git back and see the works.'

Baldwin returned to the apartment, his head in a whirl. The words, 'That nigger is bad when he drinks,' ran in his mind and sent a chill of fear for Babe shivering over him. It made him think of the loaded gun in Babe's trunk. It might be well to have it along, in case – well, just in case.

He slipped the gun into the right-hand pocket of his jacket, went down in the lift and started across town.

Babe had awakened from her heavy opium-induced sleep and felt the need of air. She went to the parlour window and opened the shutter. She looked down and saw someone who appeared very familiar to her. A man was standing near a lamp-post, and under the glare of light she saw that it was the Bearcat with his cab. There was no mistake about that.

'Hell,' she exclaimed under her breath. 'I'll never get out of here now. Who tipped him off I was here? With him followin' me now, goddam it, I'll never get nowheres.'

24

A WOMAN AND THREE MEN

HE number of the house Wayne Baldwin was looking for was in large figures that stood out clearly on the glass of the door with the light of the hallway behind it.

Yes, this was it, he told himself. What a place for her to be in! He walked up the steps cautiously. Somehow in this atmosphere he sensed the need of caution. The vestibule door was unlatched, as he had expected, for Jenny had given him every detail. He must slip by Big Ida unnoticed.

One flight up, to the right. And then – he paused at the door that opened into the flat, and listened. Then he raised his hand and knocked.

Money Johnson, hearing the knock, walked to the door, and without opening it called:

'Who's dat out dere?'

'Open that door,' Baldwin ordered him.

Johnson did not recognize the voice as that of anyone he knew or expected. He did not like the commanding tone of the caller. Baldwin knocked again.

Johnson snapped back.

'Git away fum dat door. Stop dat dere knockin'!'

The black man turned away. Baldwin stood and listened.

He heard the negro walk through the rooms. Babe and Johnson were in the alcove off the parlour. Wayne heard their voices through the thin partitions of the old house.

Money went to the parlour window to try to see the caller come out of the house.

Babe called to him.

'Is he gone? Who was it?'

It was Babe's voice, Baldwin knew. Yes, Jenny had told him the truth. Back with that nigger! It was maddening! The thought of her going back to that nigger drove him insane with jealousy.

In an uncontrollable rage Baldwin drew back a few steps in the hall and then his shoulder struck the door with a terrific impact. The door quivered and cracked. Again he hurled himself against the barrier. It still held. Then with all the force of the mounting fury in him he crashed against the door a third time. The old lock cracked under the strain and the door swung suddenly open so that Baldwin was carried headlong into the room.

Johnson stood in the centre of the floor, his eyes wild and his thick lower lip and chin stuck out. Baldwin started toward him. Then the negro, sensing that this was the white man who had come to take his woman away from him, sprang like a wild beast for Baldwin's throat.

Then about the room they careered and swayed, knocking over the furniture and striking against the walls with terrific force while Babe looked on petrified.

Baldwin's muscles, hardened by outdoor sports, began to tell on the burly negro whose soft living and carousing had weakened him. Johnson, realizing that he was rapidly losing ground, managed to break away.

He snatched up a chair to crash it down on the white man's head. But Baldwin's hand flew to his coat and he fired through the pocket. Once . . . twice . . . three times. Two of the slugs found their mark in Johnson's body. With a groan, he dropped the chair, fell back against the wall and collapsed on the floor with a sickening thud.

Babe rushed to Baldwin who was staring blankly first at the gun and then at the body on the floor.

'My God!' she cried in an awed voice. 'What have you done? What have you done?'

They stood there as Johnson's head sank lower and lower until it touched the floor. He was dead.

'Oh, why did you do it?' Babe's voice was almost a whisper.

Baldwin staggered a little. He was deathly pale. His body was wet with a cold sweat.

'I was mad – mad,' he said hoarsely, as he slumped into a chair, weak with nervous exhaustion. The gun fell from his limp hand.

They stared at each other for a moment. What were they to do? Everything seemed deadly still in the wrecked apartment. Evidently no one in the building had heard the shots fired. The racket of automobiles passing through the street and the noisy tenants had no doubt drowned out the sound. At any rate, if the shots were heard no attention had been paid to them.

Babe, half dazed, walked over to Baldwin and threw her arms around him.

'You did this for me,' she said. 'I didn't think I meant that much to you.'

She hid her face against his shoulder. She must get him out of this.

He wanted to call the police. But she insisted that he go. He protested that he couldn't leave her to face things alone. But she finally persuaded him that he could do no good by staying. She convinced him that he could help more by being free and using his money and influence than if he were arrested as the murderer. She declared that she would find some way out of it. Finally she convinced him, and, covered by the darkness, Baldwin went down the fire-escape at the rear of the flat to a yard where the remains of old cars and piles of junk lay around, and made his way out through an alley that connected with the next street.

While she had been talking to Baldwin a plan of escape had formed itself in Babe's mind. She went to the window and looked through the shutter. Yes, there was a way out.

The Bearcat was still waiting. It was almost as though fate had directed him to be there at that moment. Jenny could not know that she had done Babe the biggest favour of her life by telling the Bearcat where to find her.

Babe threw the shutter open wide and waved a part of the white curtain to attract the Bearcat's attention.

He had been studying the houses carefully and wondering which flat she might be in. He had only permitted his eyes to wander away from that row of houses for brief lengths of time.

He saw her waving now. His heart leaped with joy.

'She wants me!' he exclaimed.

Like a flash he was across the street and up the steps to the second-floor flat.

Big Ida saw him go in, but because his clothes were much like those worn by other callers at the house she paid little attention to him.

Babe had placed a chair under the knob of the door leading from the parlour into the hall. Now the lock was useless. She went to the door in the dining-room and waited for the Bearcat.

His face lighted up when he saw her standing there.

'God!' he cried. 'I've been looking all over for you. I met Jenny. She told me you was here. She gimme the street address but I forgot to get the number. I been standing out there more'n a hour.'

He spoke rapidly, nervously. Babe paid little heed to what he was saying. She closed the door after him and locked it, while he was talking. Then when she turned around he took her in his arms and kissed her.

'Gee! I'm glad to see you. I been so worried lookin' for you. But, say, ain't I lookin' swell? I'm back in shape again, honey.' Then he noticed her pallor for the first time and felt her tremble in his arms. 'Why – why, what's the matter, you're all nervous.'

Babe moved away from him a step.

'Sit down,' she said. 'Sit down a minute, dear. I want to talk to you about somethin'.'

The Bearcat gave her an anxious look.

'What's the matter, dear? Are ya sick or somethin'?' He couldn't quite make her out.

'No,' Babe said slowly. 'I'm in a lot of trouble, Bearcat. God! I don't know how to start to tell you.'

She paced the floor.

The Bearcat stood up and took her in his arms again.

'What is it? Tell me – what is it? What trouble? Tell me. Anybody doin' anythin' to you?'

She felt that she needed his strong arms around her for ever.

'I don't know how to tell you! I don't know!' She broke down then, and tears filled her eyes. It was the first time that the Bearcat had ever seen her cry.

'For God's sake, tell me!' he pleaded. 'What is it?'

Babe, with a half-hearted gesture, pointed toward the parlour.

'He's in there. He's in there.'

The Bearcat stiffened and then wheeled about and started through the bedroom toward the parlour, his eyes searching every nook and corner as he walked. The word 'he' sent a hot flush over him. He went with the one thought in his mind – 'he' – ready to kill, if he had to.

When he reached the parlour, he saw the black body in a heap on the floor. He saw a pool of blood on the carpet. And next to a chair on the floor lay a gun.

Babe had followed him and was close behind when

Bearcat made his gruesome discovery. He turned and stared at Babe.

'Who – who did this?'

Babe covered her face with her hands and swayed. He quickly took hold of her. Had she done this? Had she murdered this man?

'Good God!' he said in a hushed voice.

Babe finally collected herself, and told him a pretty story.

'I was workin' in the Five and Ten,' she began, 'and it was terribly hard there in back of that counter, dear, standing so many hours a day. Finally, I had to give it up. One of the girls from the Net was a steady customer of mine. She told me I was a fool to work so hard for a little money. She said she'd introduce me to a man who could get me a good job, with more money. The man she introduced me to was Money Johnson. A week or two passed and there was no position. He made several appointments, but nothin' ever came out of them. Once he took me out in his car, to meet a man way uptown, who was goin' to give me a job. He had three other girls along. But that meeting didn't amount to nothin' either.'

'After a few weeks of these promises and runnin' around for nothin', I had very little money left of my savings. I was forced to borrow money. Johnson loaned the money to me, saying I could pay it back when he found a job for me. He had plenty of money and loaned a lot of it out. He got his name that way.'

'But,' the Bearcat broke in, 'why didn't you let me know? Why did you borrow money from this nigger? You should've let me know. I'd have helped you.'

'I know, dear. But you had no money to spare. Besides, you was up in the camp there. And I didn't want to worry you. I wanted you to get strong again and make a comeback. Anyway – the money you got to pay for your trip – ask Joe Malone about that. Ask him where he got it to give to you.'

'Oh, Babe! You mean . . . !'

'Yes – I did it for you!'

'Oh, honey! Then you still cared for me?'

'Yes. But I had to get some more money, and Johnson was the only one I could get it from without puttin' up some kind of security. He wouldn't even take a note from me. I might've known that was kind of funny. But he was polite enough. Until – well, one time he made advances to me, but I managed to get away from him. I didn't see him for a couple of weeks. I was flat broke again. Then the other day, I got a note. It said to come up here about a job. When I saw the address I didn't like the looks of it. But I figured I'd take a chance anyway. Then when I was takin' a dress out of my trunk I saw that gun, and somethin', I don't know what, told me to take it. Warned me to take it along. So I put it in my bag.'

Babe moistened her lips and continued rapidly.

'When I got here, Money Johnson opened the door. As soon as I was inside he locked it. I could tell from the look in his eyes that it was all a frame-up. Without sayin' anything he grabbed me and ripped my dress off. See here . . .' She picked up her black lace dress, now badly torn, and showed it to the Bearcat. 'He tore it right off me – and then . . . Oh, it's too horrible to think about! He kept me here. Wouldn't let me go. I thought of the gun in my bag. But he was always watching. After a while he gave me something to drink. There must have been something in it, for I was dead to the world for hours and hours. When I woke up, it was this morning. All day he watched me so I daren't get to my bag. Then a while ago I looked out through the shutter and saw you standing down there. I thanked God for sending you to me. I couldn't cry out then, or attract your attention, for he threatened that if I screamed or tried to get away he'd kill me. Then, thinkin' he had me scared to death, he walked back through the rooms to the kitchen to get something. I saw my chance to sneak the gun out of my bag to protect myself. When he came back in here, I – I shot him!'

Babe's head sank forward, her whole body seemed penitent.

'You had a right to kill him,' the Bearcat said, his jaw tightening. 'The dirty rat! Nobody'll blame ya for shootin' him.'

Babe looked up with a wild appeal in her eyes.

'Oh, but they will, they will! When they find out I brought that gun with me, they'll say I came here with the intention of killin' him. I'll never be able to convince them different. They'll make it look like I meant to shoot him all along. Don't you see, Bearcat, I'm lost!'

The Bearcat got up like one in a dream and picked up the gun.

'Is this my gun?' he asked listlessly.

'Yes,' Babe said.

The Bearcat dropped into a chair. He wiped his face and mouth with his hand and looked at the gun. He rubbed his hands all over the weapon and then gripped it by the butt.

'I done it!' he said simply. 'I killed him! I killed him, d'you hear?'

Babe drew an inward sigh of relief. She had accomplished her purpose.

'Oh no, no! Bearcat, I couldn't – couldn't let you take the blame! I couldn't let you go through all that – for me. That's askin' too much of you!'

'No, it ain't,' he said. His voice grew firmer in his determination. 'No it ain't. I'm your husband, ain't I? I catch this guy here tryin' to attack you, an' I kill him. Why, there ain't a jury in the world that'd convict me of murder in a case like this!'

'Maybe – maybe you're right, Bearcat,' Babe said, and threw her arms around him.

'I know I'm right,' he said. 'I'll – I'll call the police now!'

'Wait, wait,' cried Babe. 'We've got to get a straight story to tell them, or the cops'll get us twisted up. How did you come to be down in the street?'

'I tried to tell you when I first came in,' he said. 'I met Jenny and she said you was here. Knowin' what kind of joints are in this row of houses, I stepped on the gas an' shot over here from 125th an' Broadway where I was parked. I got so excited thinkin' of seein' you again after so long, I didn't get the number of the house. But I knew about where it was. So I parked down there watchin' for you. Then when I seen you waving out the window I dashed up here.'

'That's it, that's it!' Bábe exclaimed excitedly. 'You see – that's the story. See how easy it is. You come home from the camp expectin' to find me workin' in the Five and Ten like when you left. I'm gone and you can't find out where I'm livin'. If they question me why I didn't let you know my address I'll have a story ready for them. Then you was lookin' around for me everywhere an' couldn't find me. You was worried. You was carryin' your gun because you was workin' late hours with your cab. You got a permit anyhow. Then to-night you meet a friend who tells you where I am. You come around to, this street but you forgot the number of the house. So you wait around thinkin' to see me come out. Then all of a sudden you see the shutter on this window fly open and spot me leaning out waving to you. Then you see someone put their hand over my mouth and drag me away from the window. You rush up here, break in the door – and catch a big nigger tearing the clothes off me. When he starts for you with murder in his eyes he picks up a chair – see that one with the leg broken off it – then you pull your gun and shoot him!' \

Babe began to laugh a little hysterically.

'That's right! That's right! See, you killed him that way! They'll believe you! They'll believe you! Call the police! Call the police! Call 'em now! See, I'll be ready!'

She sprang up and commenced to put on the torn lace

dress. It hung on her in shreds. When the cops saw that, they could have no doubt but what she had been assaulted.

The Bearcat dragged his benumbed body to the phone. He lifted the receiver and said to the operator:

'Send a policeman. There's been a murder here.'

25

THE WHEELS OF JUSTICE

BALDWIN had spent a sleepless night at the University Club. He hadn't dared to return to the Riverside Drive apartment. The more he thought of Babe the more he wanted news as to what might have happened to her. In the first editions of the morning papers he found the answer to all his questions. The screaming headlines told him the length to which Babe had gone to ensure his safety.

The scare-head of a tabloid struck him dumb with surprise.

HUSBAND SLAYS NEGRO ATTACKING WIFE

Underneath was a picture of that battered room with the body of the slain man covered with a sheet. There was also a picture of Babe and her husband, taken as they were being led to a police van.

Another headline in bold black type read:

PRIZEFIGHTER CONFESSES TO KILLING HARLEM 'POLICY KING' IN DEFENCE OF WIFE'S HONOUR

SAYS NEGRO KNOWN AS 'MONEY' JOHNSON LURED WIFE TO HARLEM FLAT WITH PROMISE OF JOB AND THEN TORE OFF HER CLOTHES.

Baldwin's eyes hastily turned to the news story that ran:

Harlem, so used to the stark comedy and tragedy of life, had a shock when it learned that 'Money' Johnson, negro 'policy king', had been shot down by a white man, whose wife Johnson lured to his rooms, and then viciously attacked.

About eleven o'clock last night, an operator in the Harlem telephone exchange called police headquarters and said that she had just received a call that someone had been murdered at No. – 127th St., in the second-floor flat at right of stairs.

Headquarters immediately notified the local precinct station and Sergeant Burke and Policeman Watson, coloured, rushed to the scene in a police car, stopping at 127th St. and Lenox Ave. to pick up Patrolman Clifford, coloured, on beat there.

Together, the officers entered the second-floor flat and there were met by a man and a woman who gave their names as George (Bearcat) Delaney, 24, a prizefighter, and Mrs. Babe Gordon Delaney, his wife. The body of a huge negro who they said was 'Money' Johnson lay in a heap on the parlour floor, dead.

Delaney admitted killing the negro, without any signs of nervousness or regret. He stated that he had accidentally learned that his wife had gone to the flat. He operated a taxicab when he was not fighting and had been separated from his wife. They had continued to be on friendly terms, however, although he had not seen her for several months until last night. A friend told him that she was seen entering the 127th St. flat.

Delaney had driven around to 127th St. in his cab, but when he arrived there he discovered that he had forgotten the number of the house. He decided to wait on the chance of seeing his wife when she came out.

Then suddenly he saw her leaning out of a window. She was waving frantically to attract his attention. Then he saw someone place a hand over her mouth and drag her back. He had a gun with him, for which he has a permit. He rushed into the house, broke in the door of the flat and found his wife struggling in the arms of a big negro, who turned to attack him when he entered. The negro attempted to crash a chair down on his head, but Delaney drew his gun and fired at him three times. Two of the bullets struck the negro, one in the stomach, and the other just under the heart.

The Medical Examiner stated that death had been almost instantaneous. The third bullet was found embedded in the wall.

While readily admitting the killing, Delaney refused to sign any statement until he first had time to consult a lawyer.

Mrs. Delaney refused to say anything except to verify her husband's story. She was wearing a black lace dress which had been literally torn to pieces in her struggle to free herself from the negro's assault.

The dead man, 'Money' Johnson, was prominent in Harlem gambling circles and had been released only a few days ago after serving three months' sentence for running a lottery in Harlem.

The explanation of the white woman's presence in Johnson's flat was that he had promised to give her a job as hostess in one of his cabarets, and had invited her there to discuss the new position. Mrs. Delaney said that she had been acquainted with him for some time, and that he had always been most courteous to her on every occasion they had met. Therefore she had not expected any trouble when she visited his apartment for the first time.

Delaney, known as the 'Bearcat' in the sport world, was at one time a contender for the middleweight championship. He was booked on a charge of homicide last night. His wife is being held as a material witness. Both will be questioned by the district attorney this morning.

Baldwin threw down the paper and leaped to his feet. He must do something. He felt it was cowardly to let this innocent man take the blame . . . for murder. But . . . after all, it wasn't his idea. Babe wanted it this way. Perhaps she was right. The disgrace to his family that would come if he gave himself up might kill his father, and it would certainly ruin his sister's life. No, this perhaps was the better way out. He could help with his money.

If the Bearcat wasn't freed, then it would be time for him to step in and tell the truth. Babe was right. Sometimes a woman sees things more clearly than a man. A selfish thought ran though his mind when he considered the Bearcat's sacrifice. How he must love Babe to do that! He wondered if this trouble would bring the two together. Jealousy again gnawed at his vitals.

He left the club, sprang into a cab and was driven across

town to the office of one of the best criminal lawyers in the city. He would at least provide Bearcat with the finest array of defence attorneys that his wealth and influence could secure.

Within a half-hour Baldwin was conferring with J. Z. Hallon, famous trial lawyer, in the latter's luxurious office overlooking Times Square. J. Z. immediately accepted the case. The Baldwin name and position were sufficient guarantee that the case was of unusual interest, not to mention the prominence given the murder in the newspapers. For J. Z. loved the limelight even more than a fat legal fee.

Within an hour, the attorney had secured a court order signed by a Supreme Court Justice for the release of Babe on twenty-five thousand dollars bail. He even visited the Bearcat in his cell to obtain the necessary details on which to build up his case.

In all this, Baldwin's name was not mentioned. He remained in the background; the Bearcat wondered why a prominent lawyer was so suddenly interested in him, and was willing to act as his counsel without a large retaining fee in advance.

The evening newspapers blazed forth with a new crop of headlines. They re-hashed the facts given in the morning editions and presented what new developments there were:

J. Z. HALLON TO CONDUCT DEFENCE OF NEGRO'S SLAYER . . . BEAUTIFUL WHITE WOMAN RESCUED FROM COLOURED SUITOR'S TORRID LOVE BY PRIZEFIGHTER HUSBAND . . . COLOURED ROMEO SLAIN IN ATTEMPT TO SEDUCE BEAUTIFUL WIFE OF BEARCAT DELANEY . . . .

Harlem's underworld is seething with resentment over the slaying of one of its own – 'Money' Johnson, 'policy king' and playboy of Strivers' Row. It is reported that Johnson's death leaves many broken hearts in the bosoms of Harlem's dusky maidens. It is thought that the nightly influx of white visitors and patrons of the black belt's pleasure resorts will be greatly curtailed to-night for fear of retaliation on the part of Johnson's henchmen and others who are enraged at the killing of one of Harlem's greatest spenders . . .

As a matter of fact, there were many in Harlem who were glad that Money Johnson was dead. Competing racketeers were well satisfied, although they chipped in large amounts of money for the magnificent funeral that was being arranged. Already, Johnson's own lieutenants were arguing over the distribution of his various interests.

Oh, de sinner man he gambled an' fell,
Oh, de sinner man he gambled an' fell,
Oh, de sinner man gambled, he gambled an' fell;
He wanted to go to hebben, but he had to go to hell,
Dere's no hidin' place down dere.

Discussion was rife in Harlem. Buzz, buzz, buzz! Liver-lips hummed and slid over useless consonants. Everywhere, morbidity fed like a vulture on the details of the murder. Everywhere, everyone knew, or thought he knew, the concealed facts of the shooting. Nigger Gert's was in a state of riot. The chorus girls of the revues sat the night through imbibing 'corn' and gin, while they pieced together all the secret, inside facts they had knowledge of. All were certain they knew the real truth of the slaying . . .

Big Ida sat with a gin bottle between her knees in Liza Jones' parlour. Every light in the flat was burning. A man had been murdered upstairs, and neither Ida nor Liza was sure they wouldn't see his ghost come walking down the stairs.

Ida took another swig of gin and wiped her eyes with a big black paw.

'Liza,' she said, 'Ah'm glad he's daid. Ef Ah couldn' hab him to love no mo', Ah'm glad he's daid. Leas'wise Ah knows wheah he is at. He ain't lovin' no white woman wheahever he is – Ah *knows* dat!'

Liza rocked back and forth in her chair.

'No. His sperit is talkin' to duh Lawd. Duh Lawd say to him: 'Money Johnson, wha' fo' yo' ain't treated Ida right? Wha' fo' yo' gwine messin' wid a white woman? Wuzn't yo' black sisters good enough fo' yo'? Ef yo' confined yo' lovin' t' duh black gals whut loved yo', yo' wouldn' be standin' heah, a-tremblin' an' a-shakin' befo' me. Gwan t' hell, sinner, till duh Day ob Judgment comes'!'

Big Ida's gin-bleared eyes rolled at Liza.

'Is dat whut duh Lawd say t' him?'

'Dat's whut duh good Lawd say.'

'Ah'm glad he's daid. Dat man ain't gwine to worry me no mo'.'

'No,' said Liza, 'he ain't gwine to worry yo' no mo', he got worries heself. Money Johnson soon be layin' down six-foot under wid Jonesy!'

'Yas,' said Ida. 'Da's all duh layin' he kin do now. Dat's gwine to be hard on him, dat low-down, dirty lovin' man!'

26

ON TRIAL

THE Black and White murder case had been played up in the newspapers for weeks before it was called to trial.

On the day the trial was to open, the morning papers bore the headline:

DELANEY DEFENCE TO INVOKE UNWRITTEN LAW

When the clerk of Part II, General Sessions, called the first juror for examination, the courtroom was packed with the intelligentsia. Authors, magazine writers, dramatists, artists, mingled with the prize-ring followers and sporting characters of Harlem.

Conspicuous in the courtroom was the black section of State witnesses.

The focus of even more attention was J. Z. Hallon and his associates, all with histories of important cases behind them. They sat with the Bearcat who appeared confident and self-assured. The jury was sworn in by the afternoon and the taking of testimony began.

One by one the State's witnesses gave their evidence, but vital testimony was lacking. The negroes told conflicting stories. On cross-examination, one or another of the defence battery confused the simple coloured witnesses about their recollection of seeing Babe with Money Johnson at such and such a time or in such and such a place.

Then the State called Cokey Jenny. But Jenny had been well taken care of beforehand. The defence saw to that. She had consented to hold her tongue for a worthy consideration. At last, good luck had come her way. She had profited immensely and all through the misfortune of Babe Gordon. What could be sweeter? Now, as she mounted the witness stand, J. Z. Hallon fixed his eyes on Jenny's face and she quaked inwardly. If she turned her eyes away they always came back to find themselves caught on the rapier-like point of J. Z.'s glance.

Her testimony was harmless, being limited to the statement that she had found out that Babe was in the 127th Street house with Johnson from Big Ida; that she had told the Bearcat that Babe was there; that she had not mentioned to the Bearcat the fact that Babe was with Johnson.

Big Ida and Liza Jones then took their turns in the witness chair. Both of them had also been bribed to a lesser extent than Jenny, but they had found it profitable to suddenly forget any incriminating evidence.

Ida testified that she had seen Johnson and Babe enter the house – Johnson first and Babe some time later. She admitted that she had felt jealous and waited all night for Babe to come out so that she could bust her up. Her testimony threw the court-room into convulsions of laughter and the judge threatened to clear the courtroom of the general public.

Liza Jones testified that she had seen neither Johnson nor Babe enter the house and wouldn't have known they were there, if Ida hadn't told her. She admitted, however, that she heard a man and woman moving around in the flat above hers, which was the one Johnson was killed in. Both she and Ida denied they had heard any noise that sounded like shots being fired.

The prosecution saw it was getting nowhere, and was willing to rest its case on the Bearcat's confession.

The defence produced two character witnesses for the Bearcat – Charlie Yates and Joe Malone, both of whom testified to the defendant's squareness, his clean living, his willingness to work hard, and his great love for his wife.

The defence concluded by putting Babe and then the Bearcat on the stand.

Babe looked ravishingly beautiful dressed all in black with a pale make-up. She took the stand and told substantially the same story of events that she had told the Bearcat the night of the murder. Her testimony was unshaken.

Then the Bearcat followed her. He told the apparently straightforward story that Babe had cooked up for him. He, too, remained unshaken by cross-examination.

On Monday morning, beginning the second week of the trial, the prosecutor summed up the State's case to the jury. He talked for about two hours. There was an adjournment for lunch, and then in the afternoon J. Z. Hallon arose and on behalf of the defendant addressed the jury. The hard light that had flashed from his eyes when he had looked at Jenny now gave place to a soft, warm, human glow. He leaned toward the jury and his voice was caressing.

'Gentlemen of the jury, you have been asked by the State to convict the defendant of murder in the first degree. Consider what that means, gentlemen. It means you are asked to condemn to death by execution in the electric chair a man who has upheld the best traditions of the white race, the honour of its womanhood.

'I do not ask you, gentlemen, to blind yourselves to the fact that the defendant has killed a man. I do not ask you to set aside the laws of the State which deal with murder. But I do ask you in the name of justice to consider in this case another law – an unwritten law, but one which is as old as the history of mankind. And that is a man's right to defend and protect the honour and virtue of his immediate family. Would any of you gentlemen hesitate to shoot down a wild beast that was attacking your wife or mother or sister? I ask you to consider this unwritten law before you condemn to ignominious death a man who had to kill in defence of his most cherished possession, a good and beautiful wife.

'The defendant, you have learned, is a clean-living, hard-working young man. You have also been told that he was forced to separate from his loving wife because of the pressure of poverty and his temporary inability to maintain a home. You have heard how his young wife, not yet twenty years of age, worked for eight hours a day behind a counter in a Five and Ten cent store, so that she should not be a financial burden to her struggling husband. Each working and saving to re-establish their little home.

'And she, out of her meagre savings, sent her husband to a training camp that he might make a comeback as a successful pugilist, while she remained in New York enduring every hardship for his sake.

'Ah, gentlemen, I ask you to meditate deeply upon the heartbreak and sacrifice involved in this living drama. And then, gentlemen, this good, adoring woman, thinking to aid her husband still further, accepted an offer of employment from a wealthy cabaret owner – a negro, 'Money' Johnson – a man who pretended to be benevolent and gentlemanly, when in reality he was a low, lustful, black beast. A man who made his money in underworld operations, a man who was released from prison but a few days before he was killed.

'This was the criminal who dared to affront the whole white world by luring to his hideaway this beautiful woman to gratify his lusts. There he kept her an unwilling prisoner, forced his brute attentions on her; tore the clothes from her body, and threatened her with a fate far worse than death to a sensitive, high-strung soul.

'And thus her husband found them. Think what must have

passed through his mind, when he burst into that room to find the wife he loved and adored, naked and helpless in the cage of that black gorilla. Think what that husband must have suffered within the space of a few seconds. The mental torture, the anguish, the supreme anger that must have consumed him at that terrible sight. And then that black vicious brute rushed to attack him with an upraised chair. There was no time for the defendant to use the fists he can wield so capably. He was mad with an anger that bordered on insanity. He had his gun with him and he fired three times at the black demon in defence of his own life and to save the woman he loved.

'I ask you, as a man to man, what would *you* have done had she been *your* wife?

'I ask you to remember that the defendant did not shoot to kill until he was first attacked by the negro, and to realize that the defendant might have based his case on a plea of involuntary manslaughter.

'But we have felt confident from the first that, when you possessed the facts, as you do now, you would not hesitate to return a verdict for acquittal. Before God, gentlemen, Delaney is not guilty.

'I appeal to your sense of honour – your pride in the woman of your race – to your intelligence – to your love of justice – and in so doing I repose in you the trust and faith of the defendant, George Delaney, and the undying gratitude of his good and beautiful wife.'

J. Z. wiped his face with a handkerchief and sat down.

The State for some unknown reason offered nothing in rebuttal. The judge read his charge to the jury and they filed out under the guard of a court officer.

In exactly twenty minutes, the foreman sent word to the judge that the jury had reached a verdict.

The jurymen filed back to their places.

The court stood up. A silence like death hung over the crowded courtroom.

The foreman's words sounded like marbles dropping in a tin basin when he announced the verdict as: 'Not Guilty.'

The Bearcat was acquitted!

Pandemonium broke loose in the courtroom. Congratulations showered on Babe and the Bearcat from all sides. Photographers snapped them in affectionate poses together. The Bearcat was jubilant and radiant. Their team-work had scored a brilliant victory.

Extras flashed out upon the street!

THE BEARCAT IS ACQUITTED! . . . PRIZEFIGHTER SCORES WIN ON UWRITTEN LAW . . . BABE AND BEARCAT HAPPY AGAIN OVER ACQUITTAL . . . BEARCAT TO TRY FOR MIDDLEWEIGHT TITLE AGAIN . . . COURTROOM CHEERS WHEN BEARCAT IS SET FREE . . .

Babe and Bearcat Delaney are now free to enjoy another honeymoon. The youngsters were too happy to discuss their future plans, but it was not denied that the Bearcat will make another attempt to win the middleweight crown. Charlie Yates, the Bearcat's former manager, says Delaney is class again, and he intends grooming him for the championship. Mrs. Bearcat says she'll see that her husband trains harder for this fight than ever before. She wants him to stage a sensational comeback in the squared circle.

27

LIFE MOVES ON

BABE and the Bearcat had faced the greatest crisis in their lives. Sitting together in the Bearcat's hotel room, Babe smiled peacefully up at him. He felt his old ring invincibility, the confident power that surges up to meet and batter down all opposition, no matter how fierce.

They were united, welded together again, Babe and himself. Perseverance had triumphed. He had won her back. The bitter heart hunger, the morbid despair, he had suffered owing to her indifference was only a memory now. He felt as he had the day he took Babe to Jersey and married her.

They were back at the Hotel Europe now. Congratulations by letter and telegram continued to arrive from everybody they had ever known. The newspapers were featuring the story of the romantic couple that had faced death's door together.

News syndicates and motion-picture companies made them offers for a true confession story of their love life.

But what heaped the measure of the Bearcat's happiness was Charlie's coming to the hotel to offer congratulations and a match with Doc Sherman as preparation for another crack at the championship.

Babe was with him continually and watched him train. The sports writers got word that the Bearcat was class again and gave him feature space, making prophecies that filled the Bearcat to the brim with confidence.

When the Bearcat stepped into the ring against Doc Sherman, he had the body of a Greek runner. Under his well-tanned skin, muscles and cords rippled in undulating grace. There was power a-plenty in bone and sinew.

Babe sat near his corner at the ringside where he could talk to her between rounds. The Bearcat knocked out Doc Sherman in the fourth round. He would fight the champion again . . .

Three days after his victory the Bearcat was alone. A week later a cablegram sent from Paris, and signed by Wayne Baldwin, notified him that Babe was arranging a divorce while she was in Europe.

Charlie was sitting beside the Bearcat, on the bed in his room at the Nelson, when a bell hop handed the cable to him. They read it together.

'Never mind, kid,' Charlie said sympathetically. 'Babe ain't the kind to stay tied to one man. She'll give this guy the air, too, before long. He's just another man in her life. He won't be the last. She's got both good and bad in her make-up, kid, and she's given you the best she's ever given any man. Buck up! You're goin' to be middleweight champeen. That ought to make it easier to stand.'

'I don't care no more, Charlie,' said the Bearcat, and there was a sob in his voice. 'I'm only glad you ain't sore at me no more. I'm only gonna think of winnin' the champeenship for you. If I can make good for you, Charlie, that's the best feelin' I'll ever have. That's all I want now. I know I ain't enough for Babe. I guess – I guess she was just too beautiful for me. Like a dream, y'know, Charlie, that's gone when you wake up. It won't be so hard doin' wit'out her now. Seems like I'm used to doin' wit'out her. I love her though, Charlie! How I love her! I'll always love her . . . '

The Bearcat buried his face in the pillow, to hide from Charlie the tears that trickled down his cheeks.

Babe is in Paris now with Wayne Baldwin, and they are happy together. But what of the days when the glamour of that gay city has won off? What will happen when Babe meets another man who appeals to her senses more than Baldwin, or possibly has far greater wealth? It will be the old, old story over again. Even if she decides to marry Baldwin, that would not prevent her having a lover, or lovers, on the side. That is Babe Gordon. That is her life. Nothing can change her. She isn't even certain she will not slip away to-morrow to a rendezvous with some Paris apache whom she has seen the night before. Nothing is certain about Babe Gordon except her desire . . . And that desire she will find the means of gratifying as long as she is young. After that . . . but Babe lives too intensely in the present to consider the future.

As for Baldwin, the frequent sight of black and white mingling together in Paris brings always the memory of Johnson's face when he had shot him. He cannot avoid thinking of Babe's white body and Johnson's black body, darkness mating with dawn. It is terrible, and yet it gives him a sensual thrill like the one he received when he first saw Babe and the black man in the Harlem Breakfast Club. He has Babe now to himself. He is happy. But the black and white pattern is indelibly woven into the tapestry of his memory. He will never forget . . .